PRAISE FOR M. L. BUCHMAN

3x Top 10 Romance of the Year

— ALA BOOKLIST

Tom Clancy fans open to a strong female lead will clamor for more.

— DRONE, PUBLISHERS WEEKLY

(Miranda Chase is) one of the most compelling, addicting, fascinating characters in any genre since the Monk television series.

— DRONE, ERNEST DEMPSEY

(*Drone* is) the best military thriller I've read in a very long time. Love the female characters.

— SHELDON MCARTHUR, FOUNDER OF THE MYSTERY BOOKSTORE, LA

Superb!

— DRONE, BOOKLIST, STARRED REVIEW

A fabulous soaring thriller.

— TAKE OVER AT MIDNIGHT, MIDWEST
BOOK REVIEW

Meticulously researched, hard-hitting, and suspenseful.

— PURE HEAT, PUBLISHERS WEEKLY,
STARRED REVIEW

The first…of (a) stellar, long-running (military) romantic suspense series.

— THE NIGHT IS MINE, BOOKLIST, THE
20 BEST ROMANTIC SUSPENSE NOVELS:
MODERN MASTERPIECES

Expert technical details abound, as do realistic military missions with superb imagery that will have readers feeling as if they are right there in the midst and on the edges of their seats.

— LIGHT UP THE NIGHT, RT REVIEWS, 4
1/2 STARS

Buchman has catapulted his way to the top tier of my favorite authors.

— FRESH FICTION

M L. Buchman's ability to keep the reader right in the middle of the action is amazing.

— LONG AND SHORT REVIEWS

The only thing you'll ask yourself is, "When does the next one come out?"

— WAIT UNTIL MIDNIGHT, ROMANTIC
TIMES BOOK REVIEWS, 4 STARS

I knew the books would be good, but I didn't realize how good.

— NIGHT STALKERS SERIES, KIRKUS
REVIEWS

THE COMPLETE HOTSHOTS

A WILDFIRE ROMANCE SHORT STORY
COLLECTION

M. L. BUCHMAN

Buchman Bookworks

Other works by M. L. Buchman: *(* - also in audio)*

Thrillers

Dead Chef
Swap Out!
One Chef!
Two Chef!

Miranda Chase
*Drone**
*Thunderbolt**
*Condor**

Romantic Suspense

Delta Force
*Target Engaged**
*Heart Strike**
*Wild Justice**
*Midnight Trust**

Firehawks
MAIN FLIGHT
Pure Heat
Full Blaze
*Hot Point**
*Flash of Fire**
Wild Fire
SMOKEJUMPERS
*Wildfire at Dawn**
*Wildfire at Larch Creek**
*Wildfire on the Skagit**

The Night Stalkers
MAIN FLIGHT
The Night Is Mine
I Own the Dawn
Wait Until Dark
Take Over at Midnight
Light Up the Night
Bring On the Dusk
By Break of Day

AND THE NAVY
Christmas at Steel Beach
Christmas at Peleliu Cove
WHITE HOUSE HOLIDAY
*Daniel's Christmas**
*Frank's Independence Day**
*Peter's Christmas**
*Zachary's Christmas**
*Roy's Independence Day**
*Damien's Christmas**
5E
Target of the Heart
Target Lock on Love
Target of Mine
Target of One's Own

Shadow Force: Psi
*At the Slightest Sound**
*At the Quietest Word**

White House Protection Force
*Off the Leash**
*On Your Mark**
*In the Weeds**

Contemporary Romance

Eagle Cove
Return to Eagle Cove
Recipe for Eagle Cove
Longing for Eagle Cove
Keepsake for Eagle Cove

Henderson's Ranch
*Nathan's Big Sky**
*Big Sky, Loyal Heart**
*Big Sky Dog Whisperer**

Love Abroad
Heart of the Cotswolds: England
Path of Love: Cinque Terre, Italy

Other works by M. L. Buchman:

Contemporary Romance (cont)

Where Dreams
Where Dreams are Born
Where Dreams Reside
Where Dreams Are of Christmas
Where Dreams Unfold
Where Dreams Are Written

Science Fiction / Fantasy

Deities Anonymous
Cookbook from Hell: Reheated
Saviors 101

Single Titles
The Nara Reaction
Monk's Maze
the Me and Elsie Chronicles

Non-Fiction

Strategies for Success
Managing Your Inner Artist/Writer
*Estate Planning for Authors**
Character Voice
*Narrate and Record Your Own Audiobook**

Short Story Series by M. L. Buchman:

Romantic Suspense

Delta Force
Delta Force

Firehawks
The Firehawks Lookouts
The Firehawks Hotshots
The Firebirds

The Night Stalkers
The Night Stalkers
The Night Stalkers 5E
The Night Stalkers CSAR
The Night Stalkers Wedding Stories

US Coast Guard
US Coast Guard

White House Protection Force
White House Protection Force

Contemporary Romance

Eagle Cove
Eagle Cove

Henderson's Ranch
*Henderson's Ranch**

Where Dreams
Where Dreams

Thrillers

Dead Chef
Dead Chef

Science Fiction / Fantasy

Deities Anonymous
Deities Anonymous

Other
The Future Night Stalkers
Single Titles

CONTENTS

INTRODUCTION

The Firehawks Hotshots aren't directly tied to the Firehawks of my fictional Mount Hood Aviation. And yet they were born from those stories.

There are many different elements to a wildland firefight:

- Lookouts
- Spotter aircraft (which have replaced most lookouts and are now in turn being replaced by satellites detecting atypical heat blooms)
- Local fire departments (often with wildfire engines)
- Hotshots who hike into the firefight
- Smokies who parachute in
- Helitack (firefighters delivered by helicopter)
- Air tankers (which include helicopters and fixed-wing aircraft)

Then, especially on the big fires, there are whole layers of camps, support, and command-and-control teams. A really big fire may mobilize more people than lived in the town I grew up in (1,200). The hotshots are only the tiniest slice of the battle and my stories are but a tiny slice of that team's view.

In writing about the MHA Firehawks, I slowly learned about these other types of teams and wanted to learn more. What better excuse than to write a series of romance stories about them? And that's how the Firehawks Hotshots came into being.

They are technically an IHC—Interagency Hotshot Crew—who can be called up by the Bureau of Land Management, US Forest Service, and others, hence the Interagency part of their name. They are typically formed by one of the agencies, but may also be formed by local fire departments. These teams assemble every spring and mostly disband every winter after the fire season is over. Traveling all over the western US in the "Box" as their truck is called, they fight fires wherever they occur, typically May to October.

Sixteen hour days, sleeping wild, and eating camp food is the norm. Working forty-eight hours or more straight is not the exception when the fires are raging.

Some areas have such horrible fire seasons that those teams rarely travel out of state: California, Oregon, Washington, Idaho, and Montana. Others have a very short but intense season, in say Arizona or New Mexico, then travel farther afield. They are often on the road for months.

I set my team in the Washington Cascade Mountains for several reasons: there is no real-life team based there, I love the area, and I saw the results of a horrible fire that swept through the region years ago.

But it really came from Candace. She was so excited to form her own team, that I had to write her story.

FIRE LIGHT FIRE BRIGHT

Candace Cantrell *fights forest fires as a lead member of a hotshot crew. When she lands the opportunity to build a brand new crew of her own, she ends up with more than she bargained for.*

Former Navy SEAL Luke Rawlings *struggles with a past he can't leave behind. A past that blinds him to the future, until the moment he tries out for a new hotshot crew.*

Most people wish upon a star. Hotshot crews do it differently:

"Fire Light Fire Bright…"

INTRODUCTION

IHC, Interagency Hotshot Crews, are one of the backbones of wildland firefighting. Yet they were largely unknown to the general public prior to the disaster at the 2013 Yarnell Hill Fire in which nineteen members of the twenty-person Granite Mountain Hotshots crew were killed in a single burnover. Their position was overrun and, despite deploying fire shelters, the manzanita burned so hot that it melted the foil shelters (well past 1,500 degrees —three times the heat that a home oven can produce and on a multi-acre scale). I can highly recommend the movie *Only the Brave,* though it was made long after these stories were written.

These teams drive as close to fires as possible and then hike in. Often with minimal support, they are the ground team that directly confronts the blaze. A smokejumper is only called on the worst fires or when there is no other way to reach the fire quickly from the ground. A local fire department isn't equipped or trained to handle a large wildfire—between local fire and the elite smokejumpers is the gap that IHCs walk into.

Hotshots cut a brush-free line with chainsaws and specialized axes called Pulaskis (axe on one side, adze on the other—essentially a sharpened hoe). They shovel dirt over flames to put out the fire and they dig up hotspots so they can drown them with portable pumps using inch-and-a-half hoses before the embers flare up and reignite a tinder-dry forest. They even use fire in controlled backfires to rob the main fire of its fuel—truly fighting fire with fire.

When Candace insisted that she wanted to start her own IHC, who was I to argue.

I found Luke easily enough. After researching so many active military scenarios for my other series, it was time to start telling the stories of those whose service hadn't ended by choice. The first wounded warrior I wrote was Lois Lang in *NSDQ* (*Night Stalkers Don't Quit*). She had lost her foot, whereas Luke had lost something deep inside.

I love the contrast of a woman so sure of herself, helping a man who once was. They would remain the heart of the team for the rest of the short story series, something I always enjoy.

"Hi, I'm Candace Cantrell. First Rule: anyone who calls me Candy, who isn't my dad," she hooked a thumb at Fire Chief Carl Cantrell standing at-ease beside her, "is gonna get my boot up their ass. We clear on that?"

A rolling mumble of "Yes, ma'am." "Clear." and "Got it, Candace." rippled back to her from the recruits. Some answered almost as softly as the breeze working its way up through the tall pines. Others trumpeting it out as if to get her notice. A few offered simple nods.

She surveyed the line of recruits slowly. Way too early to make any judgments, but it was tempting. Day One, Minute One, and she could already guess five of the forty applicants weren't going to make it into the twenty slots she had open.

The one thing they all, including her dad, needed to see right up front was their team leader's complete confidence. Candace had been fighting wildfires for the U.S. Forest Service hotshot teams for a decade. She'd worked her way up to foreman twice, and had been gunning for a shot at superintendent of a whole twenty-person crew when her dad had called.

"We're got permission to form up an IHC in the heart of the Okanagan-Wenatchee National Forest," he never was long on greetings over the phone.

Her mouth had watered. A brand new Interagency Hotshot Crew didn't happen all that often.

"I talked to the other captains and we want you to form it up."

Now her throat had gone dry and she had to fight to not let it squeak.

"Me?"

"You aren't gonna let me down now, Candy Girl?"

"You shittin' me?" Not a chance.

Then he'd hit her with that big belly laugh of his.

"Knew you'd like the idea."

And simple as that, she'd been out of the San Juan IHC at the end of the Colorado fire season and back home in the Cascade Mountains of Washington State. She'd grown up in the resort town of Leavenworth—two thousand people and a ka-jillion tourists. The city fathers had transformed the failing timber town into a Bavarian wonderland back in the sixties. But that didn't stop the millions of acres of the National Forest and the rugged sagebrush-steppe ecosystem further east in central Washington from torching off every summer.

The very first thing she'd done, before she'd even left the San Juan IHC, was to call in a pair of ringers as her two foremen. Jess was short, feisty, and could walk up forested mountains all day with heavy gear without slowing down a bit. Patsy was tall, quiet, and tough. Candace had them stand in with the crews for the first days because she wanted their eyes out there as well.

"Second, see that road?" she asked the recruits and

pointed to the foot of National Forest Road 6500. She'd had their first meet-up be here rather than at the fire hall in town. A gaggle of vehicles were pulled off the dirt of Little Wenatchee River Road. Beater pickups dominated, but there were a couple of hammered Civics, a pair of muscle cars, and a gorgeous Harley Davidson that she considered stealing it was so sweet.

The recruits all looked over their shoulders at the one lane of dirt.

"We're going for a stroll up that road. We leave in sixty seconds."

Like a herd of sheep, they all swung their heads to look at her.

"Fifty-five seconds, and this ain't gonna be a Sunday stroll."

You could tell the number of seasons they'd fought fire just by their reactions.

Five or more? They already wore their boots. Daypacks with water and energy bars were kept on their shoulders during her intro. And despite it being Day One of the ten-day shakedown, all had some tools: fold-up shovel and a heavy knife strapped to their leg at a minimum. Only she, Jess, and Patsy had Pulaski wildland fire axes tied to their gear, but all the veterans knew the drill.

Three to four seasons? Groans and eyerolls. Packs were on the ground beside them. No tools, but they knew what was coming now that she'd told them—ten kilometers, at least, and not one meter of it flat.

One to two seasons? Had the right boots on, but no packs. They were racing back to their vehicles to see what equipment they could assemble.

Rookies? Tennis shoes, ball caps, no gear, blank stares.

"Forty-five seconds, rooks. Boots and water. If you're

not on the trail in fifty seconds, you're off the crew." That got their asses moving.

There was one man on the whole crew she couldn't pigeonhole, the big guy who'd climbed off the Harley. His pack and the fold-up shovel strapped to it were so new they sparkled. But his boots and the massive hunting knife on his thigh both showed very heavy use.

A glance at her Dad's assessing gaze confirmed it. Something was odd about the Harley man and his easy grin. Not rugged handsome, but still very nice to look at. Powerful shoulders, slim waist. Not an athlete's build, but rather someone who really used his body. His worn jeans revealed that he already had the powerful legs that every hotshot would develop from endless miles of chasing fire over these mountains and steppes for the next six months. It was like he was a Hollywood movie: some parts of him were so very right, but a lot of the details were dead wrong.

---

2

*L*uke Rawlings looked at the team superintendent. Couldn't help himself, 'cause damn she was a treat to look at. Her white-blond hair was short and sassy, her body was seriously fit, but curved like a sweet-Candy dream girl. Her no-nonsense attitude just cracked him up; he could hear that natural state of command that you only learned the hard way, by doing it. Not something he'd ever expected to find in a hot civilian babe.

When he'd mustered out, SEAL Lieutenant Commander Altman had suggested he try firefighting. Altman was a smart dude, so Luke had followed his suggestion. He'd kicked around with a big city fire department doing ride-alongs for a while. Chicago Fire were all super guys and they kept trying to sign him aboard, but tramping pavement and cement, doing fire inspections for date tags on commercial fire extinguishers…he'd rather be back in the African jungle. If his nerves would let him, which he so wasn't going to think about now.

He still wasn't sure how he'd heard about the hotshot crews, but walking into a wildfire—he just liked the way it sounded.

And looking at "Not Candy" Cantrell, he was damn glad he'd followed his whim and ridden his Harley west. "Not Candy." What did that make her? Cake, or main course?

She moved to the head of the dirt forest road where it left the pavement. The old hands had already moved onto the track, but they waited once there. So, hotshot teams moved as a unit. Good. That was familiar.

He dropped into line to watch. Candace had already picked out at least two of her team, he could see the surreptitious communication between the three of them; all three with worn fireaxes, despite it being just a training walk.

Number One tool of their trade. Got it.

So, her recruit assessment was underway from the inside as well. The two insiders were watching the rookies, but the superintendent also had her eye tracking him.

Didn't require his kind of training to catch the glance between father and daughter as they assessed him. Let them wonder. There were some things he'd rather not talk about. He was just gonna play Mr. Average Joe Firefighter Hopeful and see how it rolled.

3

Day Five and Candace was halfway through the selection process. She'd been right on four out of the five who'd been gone on Day One; one had made it to Day Two. She'd lost five more since then. She was down from forty to thirty on her way to the final twenty to be accepted into the crew.

She knew crew bosses who did it solely with physical testing: massive hikes, hard calisthenics, and so on. She preferred to incorporate as much training as possible. *Here's what the real world will be like, kids. You up for it?*

Yesterday she had them clearing a line. When a fire was working its way through the forest duff and detritus, it was up to a hotshot team to scrape and clear a wide swath down to mineral soil, and to do it in lines often a mile or more long. Upslope and down.

Hotshots might be the elite ground crew, barely a step down from the smokejumpers, but they spent a lot of time grubbing dirt lines. Sixteen hours she'd kept them at it, sunup to well past sundown, finishing by headlamp, then sacking out right where they were. On a big fire, they'd be going twenty-four to thirty-six hours at a time and she wanted to give them a taste of that. They all wore field packs now and either a Pulaski axe or a McLeod rake. Unlike most field duty during the season, her dad's townie crew did roll in with a wildfire engine loaded up for each meal; so at least they ate well.

Today, she pulled Jess and Patsy out of the crowd and introduced them around the deep woods camp as her two foremen. She'd left them in the team long enough that their exceptional skills and experience had become standout obvious, so there were no hard feelings about having spies in their midst. At least none that she could spot.

Luke Rawlings had offered her one of his enigmatic smiles that seemed to say, *About time.* As if he'd known about them since the first day.

She was half tempted to boot the man, just because the puzzle of him was so damned distracting. Candace needed the team to stay focused and this man was a complete aberration. But the part of her that he was sidetracking had nothing to do with forest fires, so she did her best to ignore that and left him in place.

He clearly had no experience with wildfire or hotshot techniques, but show him something once and he had it solid. Not just what to do, but like he'd always had it. Luke had clearly never run a chainsaw, didn't even know how to start one. Yet after a single day that the team had spent clearing some new land for a farmer downslope near the town of Monitor, he moved like a three-year sawyer.

And he never spoke much. Strong and silent type. "Just takin' care of business, ma'am" attitude. When he did speak, his voice had a soft southern to it, Tennessee or Kentucky—that he clearly knew was a total charmer. Of the six women among the recruits, four had already taken a run at him. As far as Candace could tell, not a one of them had gotten past that polite shield.

What are you hiding, Rawlings?

He wasn't saying. Well, today should separate out more of the recruits. Question was, did she want him separated out or not?

She moved them downslope from where they'd camped —an uncomfortable site on the slopes of Dragontail Peak. Anyone who thought fires didn't burn on this kind of terrain, so hotshots never walked it, would be disabused of that notion over the fast-approaching fire season.

When they reached a small clearing, her Dad had already arrived with a wildfire engine. These trucks were wide, heavy, and smaller than the standard in-town engines. More the size of a utility service truck, they could cross surprisingly rough terrain with a great deal of gear and five hundred gallons of water.

Once they were gathered, Candace pulled out a fire shelter pouch and held it up for all to see.

"This is a five-hundred dollar device of last resort. You will always have one on your hip and you will protect it more carefully than your own face. If everything else goes wrong and you find yourself in a burnover situation, this foil shelter is your only chance of survival."

That sobered a number of their faces.

"Today, we'll practice with plastic shelters worth about ten dollars. I don't want to see even the smallest tear or nick in these, because if it's a real fire, fifteen hundred degree flame will find its way right through that gap and toast your ass. I can't begin to tell you how much paperwork that will cause me."

That got her some good laughs. Even the old hands appreciated the dark humor of it. She knew that at least three of them besides herself had ridden out a burnover under a shelter. And several of them had friends among the Yarnell 19 who died in 2013; the manzanita-fed flames too hot for even the foil shelters' protection.

Luke Rawlings, however, looked at her as if she'd just committed a crime against humanity. His expression had gone dark enough that she suddenly feared for her safety.

No. It wasn't her he was looking at.

He was looking at something that wasn't in the grass clearing, but rather in his past. Well, she pitied whoever had put that look on his face, because she'd wager they hadn't survived long after whatever they'd done to piss him off.

She made it a policy to not pull a recruit's application file during the ten-day trial, but she'd broken down last night. U.S. Navy Chief Petty Officer Luke Rawlings, retired. That explained some things, but not others. She'd fought fire beside plenty of ex-soldiers before, though none as quietly competent as Rawlings. Many hadn't been able to face the fire itself when it came down to reality: some froze, some ran, and one got the shakes so bad they had to medevac him out.

Luke was steady. Always helping the rawest rookies get their feet under them with a gentle word and a clear demonstration. Infinitely patient, he kept working with them until they really had it. He'd be a good man to have around.

Erase that, Cantrell. Mr. Ex-Navy Luke Altman would be a good *firefighter* to have around. She just wished she could stop thinking about the *man* who watched her as much as she was watching him.

Usually about half of the former soldiers would be weeded out by the fire shelter deployment exercise.

It was something of a surprise when she realized that she really hoped Luke wasn't one of those.

eep breathing barely pulled Luke back from the edge.

Pine scent.

Not jungle.

Dry air.

Better.

He'd been civilian for six months now, and no day was easier. *The only easy day was yesterday!* He kept repeating the SEAL motto to himself, but it wasn't helping. "Yesterday" had totally sucked as well.

There was no way to predict when it was going to slap him; half his team gone between one breath and the next.

They'd been deep in the Democratic Republic of the Congo having a quiet moment in a quiet town. The woman had strolled by where they were eating lunch with a basket of melons balanced on her head. The brightly-colored flowing *kanga* had hidden only parts of her fine form; the part that had been five kilos of explosives. The blast had ripped her, half his team, and one whole end of a Congolese market to shreds.

He did his best to focus on Candace Cantrell's lecture about how to deploy a fire shelter.

Breathe in the dry pine.

Piece by piece he forced his brain back together.

Only easy day was yesterday.

U.S. soil, not the Congo.

Training here—way easier than any single day of BUD/S.

Essential survival techniques that didn't include flak vests and Kevlar helmets. Weapons of the forest were a Pulaski tool and a chainsaw, not an M-249 SAW machine gun and Barrett M107 sniper rifle.

Luke dug the toe of his boot into the thick mountain bunch grass, appreciating Candace's steady manner and calm voice. Getting easily lost in it. She'd been growing more and more crucial to his daily control, his well being.

Anyone who'd served and said that each day wasn't a massive struggle was only lying to himself. But being around Candace made that struggle seem worthwhile.

That thought finally kicked him all the way out of his downloop and left him blinking at her in surprise.

She was important to him.

How the hell had that happened?

Women were…not like her. It's like she was a different breed or species or something. A better one.

Some part of his brain, trained by far too many officer harangues, had kept up with the lecture. She now stood close enough that he could smell her—like sweet honey and glacier-fed streams—as she had him stepping into the shelter, pulling it up over his back and his head, and lying down with his face in a hole dug into the dirt.

"Keep your face in the hole, it's where the air is coolest," Candace called out loud enough to be heard easily through the shelter. "Feet to the fire. Your team leader may call out a last moment shift. If so, you keep your face in the hole and rotate your feet around. Do not, I repeat, do not lift the edge of your shelter. That is a life-and-death decision. The edges stay down even when you think you'll go mad."

Great! Just what Luke needed, another reason to lose it.

"Fire is loud. Freight train loud. It will try to rip away your shelter. Don't let it."

And then all hell broke loose.

His shelter slapped down on him!

A thunderclap of noise!

He was back in battle! God, no!

He fought the urge to scream.

Struggled for focus.

Orders.

His commander had said to hold fast. To stay down. Under cover. He gripped the edges of his shelter harder than he'd clutched the stock of his MP5N machine pistol as he was blown backward into a goat merchant's stall. Gripped so hard he wondered that his fingers didn't break.

He heard a voice yelling out, "Stay under the shelter!" Candace's voice.

The blast moved away, battered another shelter nearby, returned! Then moved off again. It was…the spray of a fire hose off the wildfire engine. Water began to trickle under the edge of the shelter.

Shit.

Not a bomb.

Not a war.

He racked in a painful breath. Just a test with water. No cracked ribs this time, he could breathe. He started laughing…then crying. Mickey, Ralph, Doug; shooting the shit over Ndakala fish curry one second and scattered in pieces the next.

Water flowed under the edge of the shelter and he couldn't stop it.

Couldn't stop it as it flowed out of his eyes as well.

For the first time in the year since he'd lost them, he wept into his dirt hole in the ground as the cleansing water washed over and under him inside the safety of his little shelter.

A woman's voice kept calling to him that it would all be okay, just stay safe.

andace sat at the edge of the grass clearing, outside the circle of firelight, and watched the final twenty sitting around the campfire. Day Ten, they'd made it. And just as importantly, so had she. The Leavenworth IHC was happening.

Dad and the department's mostly volunteer crew had delivered hotdogs and burgers with all the trimmings, massive bags of chips, and local craft beer. The whole team's laughter had that easy confidence of a crew who'd formed up well.

She really had done it.

Another three weeks of serious training and she'd list the team as ready for call out. They'd done a carefully controlled prescribed burn on Day Eight and not a one of them had flinched, which boded well. The only test left was one she couldn't arrange, facing an angry wildfire on the run. That final trial she'd have to leave up to the whim of Mother Nature and the needs of the U.S. Forest Service.

"Thinking pretty hard there, Cantrell." Luke handed

her a fresh beer then waved his own at the spot beside her, asking permission before he sat on the grass.

"I do that sometimes," she nodded for him to join her. He did, stretching out his legs and leaning back on his elbows, but not too close. That southern gentleman. Another thing that made him such a standout from normal guys.

Having sought her out, he remained silent.

"Something shifted for you during the training. Something big." When he'd gone under the shelter, she'd thought she was going to lose him for sure, but when he'd emerged…

His shrug was noncommittal. Guy speak for *maybe*.

"All your pieces fit."

"Say what?" That got his attention away from the team around the campfire to studying her closely out here in the shadows.

"When you first showed up, it's like you were fractured. All made up of different pieces that didn't really fit together. That's gone now."

Again that long quiet study. She didn't turn to face him. Couldn't. A team was just that, especially when you were the leader. By season's end, these people would be as close as brothers and sisters—to her, to each other. But Luke Rawlings made her wish for different things. Things she'd rather he didn't see.

"Pretty forthright there."

His accusation was accurate so she didn't waste time denying it.

He turned to watch the fire once more.

She hoped she hadn't scared him off. Though he didn't look like a man who scared easily.

"You remind me of my last commander. Lieutenant Commander Altman was about as straight ahead as they come."

"Is that a compliment?"

"You have no idea, lady. Compliments don't come any higher. And SEAL commanders don't come any better than Altman."

"You're a SEAL?" she finally turned to look at him and discovered his dark eyes studying her from close by.

"Past tense."

"No wonder you're so damn good at everything. Besides, is there such a thing as a past tense SEAL?"

He grimaced, "Not really."

She'd never met— "I've never met anyone like you. You just seem so—" safe. A job didn't get much less safe than leading an Interagency Hotshot Crew, no matter that safety was their number one priority. "—so…Shit!" Words were failing her beneath his dark gaze.

"Never met a woman like you either 'Not Candy' Cantrell." His deep voice was a little rough. "Can't seem to stop thinking about you. Even invading my damned dreams." He looked disgusted.

"Wet ones, Mr. SEAL?"

His easy laugh wrapped around them both acknowledging the pun and the way she'd learned to deal with that line head on.

"White dress ones, lady."

Candace could feel herself freezing up. Yet another man who thought she belonged in some neat bride-wifely pigeonhole. So not her.

"White dress made of Nomex," Luke mused half to himself. "How's that for an amazing image?"

Nomex was the material used in making fire gear, became a second skin to a hotshot. Luke dreamed of her as a firefighter? Every man she'd ever been with had tried to talk her out of it. To him, or at least his subconscious, it was an integral part of her. Something no one else except her father had ever understood.

She'd never been a big one on dreams, never remembered the ones at night, or made up ones during the day. But she couldn't deny that she'd had her eye, and her thoughts, on Luke Altman since the day he'd stepped off his big Harley and joined the hotshot trials.

She could feel him watching her by the warm shadows of firelight. Quiet like a SEAL and patient like a gentleman. Strong enough to sweep her away and safe enough that she'd never think he'd do something without permission.

Turning to study him, she did her best to look inside herself, never one of her strengths.

Did she want to grant that permission?

Big time.

Well, he'd called you forthright as a compliment, so what are you waiting on?

Nothing.

Candace leaned down to kiss him.

After an initial grunt of surprise, he proved that cutting down trees and digging soil weren't the only things he was exceptionally skilled at. She melted against his heat until they both groaned together.

She could feel their smiles start in that instant and continue to grow. When it threatened to turn into laughter of sheer joy, she moved back until she too was resting against the soft grasses on her elbows and facing the campfire and the celebrating crews.

So, her heart wanted to race as fast as his Harley?

She'd let it.

"Going to be an interesting summer, Mr. Hotshot," Candace did her best to keep her tone casual as the heat continued to ripple deliciously through her body.

"I'm thinking it could be a whole lot more than one of them…" he paused long enough for her to turn and see his smile, "…Sweet Candy Fire."

Candace turned back to the fire, but could feel her smile going goofy.

She was thinking exactly the same thing.

FIRELIGHTS OF CHRISTMAS

Patsy Jurgen's *first season as foreman of a wildfire hotshot crew burns up her nervous energy. She fights to do her best for her crew and to create the firefighting career she always dreamed of. Falling in love? An unwanted distraction.*

Sam Parker *bought the bakery in the mountain resort town of Leavenworth, Washington. He intends to bury all memory of his last relationship in an avalanche of Bavarian treats. Woman-free? Definitely the way to go.*

But neither of them counted on the heat of the Firelights of Christmas.

INTRODUCTION

This was my first story character who was inspired by another short story rather than a novel. I hadn't yet realized that I was writing a short story series about hotshots rather than just a story or two about them. Actually at the time I wrote this I had written less than a dozen short stories…ever. And never before had I thought of a short story series at all.

But merely being the boss' assistant wasn't enough for Patsy Jurgen and she demanded her own story, in her quiet yet *very* insistent way.

And with December fast approaching, a Christmastime setting seemed eminently sensible. It wasn't a long stretch to incorporate one of my wife's favorite year-round Christmas stores. The one in the heart of Leavenworth, Washington is fantastic.

Leavenworth was just another struggling mountain town when its citizens decided to reconceive itself as a Bavarian resort. The town's architecture was restructured in a timber-and-white-stucco style. A village square was formed, complete with a gazebo for a brass quartet playing

Christmas carols. The massive investment paid off hugely. Rather than dying off like so many former timber towns, this one has thrived in its remote mountain fastness.

When we lived closer, we'd make a special trip there to purchase that year's new ornament and wander the snow-filled streets. A dinner of bratwurst with a stein of beer was, of course, in order.

It is also a town that attracts people ready to step back from the big city pressures of Seattle. Hence, Patty finds her baker.

1

———————

"Rise and shine," Patsy Jurgen swept down the hall of the Cascade Hotshots barracks. This was their first wildland firefighting season, the newest hotshot team in the country. And the worn-out, board-and-batten building was their new home. She thumped the side of her fist once on each wooden door, making them rattled loudly on old hinges.

She smiled to herself. It had taken her six years to make foreman of an Interagency Hotshot Crew and this was about the nicest place she'd ever lived. She'd heard some of the new recruits griping good-naturedly about a "hardship post." Once the fire season hit, they wouldn't be in residence here in Leavenworth, Washington all that often. And after their first month or so walking to the wildfires, they'd bless having running water, a cot, and a roof that only leaked a little.

After two weeks of recruit selection and three more of intense training, the twenty hotshots had really come together. The old hands and the new were blending well.

They had yet to be tested by anything more strenuous than a prescribed burn to cut fuel levels in untended fields around the mountain town, but she knew the real thing would be happening all too soon.

Not soon enough for her.

Candace Cantrell's phone call that she was forming up the Cascade IHC had brought Patsy running. Cantrell had been a kick-ass foreman on the San Juan IHC and Patsy wanted to lead her own crew someday. She couldn't ask for a better slot that being Cantrell's foreman, her Number Two. Of course she had to share that particular slot, one super and two foremen to a crew.

Jess Monroe, the other foreman, opened his barrack door before she could thump it.

"Yeah, yeah! I'm up already, Jurgen." He didn't look it, but she knew from overlapping him on various crews over the years that he wasn't a morning person and the only thing that really woke him up fast was a fire. He wore shorts, and nothing else. He was hotshot fit, muscle rippled along his legs and chest.

"Day one, Monroe." Candace had just informed her team last night that she'd let the Forest Service know the Cascade IHC was ready for call out. A real testament to her skill as a superintendent that they'd trained up so fast, because Patsy agreed. They were ready.

"Day one," he looked down at his watch. "Still early yet. Wanna come in and celebrate?" He held the door a little wider. As foreman, he had a room to himself instead of a two-bunk, just as she did.

"I think you're still dreaming, Jess." The man would flirt with a burning tree. He never pushed; teasing women was just some kind of a game to him. Most flirted back and they all seemed to have fun with it. A skill she'd never had nor wanted. She reached out and pulled his door shut —with him on one side and her on the other.

It wasn't *that* early. She'd woken everyone just early enough to ease into it and eat before the day's planned exercise.

Candace and Luke Rawlings, one of the newest recruits, had gotten a small apartment also close by the fire station. The heat between them was amazing to watch; it was just so…right. Candace had always been deadly serious about hotshotting; fire chief's daughter, no big surprise. But with Luke she glowed like, well, like she was happy.

Patsy hadn't seen that one coming at all. Candace was so dedicated to wildfire that she had become a role model for Patsy. Her suddenly finding love was like a crack in Patsy's worldview—one she still didn't know what to do with.

Patsy had woken before sunrise, an old habit, and gone outside to watch the day break before waking the others. The sun had lit the towering peaks of the Cascade Mountains which climbed up to the west of Leavenworth eventually topping out at Stevens Pass. The line of sunlight had moved down the conifer and gray rock-covered slopes like the slice of a knife, the line was so clean. To the east, the mountains fell away into hills headed for the rolling sagebrush and orchard steppes of Eastern Washington.

On the silent air, broken only by a blue jay's call, the scent of pine washed through the river valley. Dry pine. It was only June, but already she knew it was going to be a hot summer and a busy fire season. They'd been smart to sponsor a hotshot crew here.

Now that everyone was awake, but not moving yet, she was suddenly at loose ends. So she walked the couple blocks into the sleeping town; hadn't had a moment to breathe during training to give it the once over. All of her prior postings had been pretty far out into the nothing. "Town" usually meant a church, a grocery store that was also a gas station, and a pizza joint that was more importantly the sole bar. But here, the Cascade hotshots had been formed by Chelan County and posted in a resort town surrounded by towering timber.

Leavenworth was…bizarre. A failing timber town in the 1950s, it had resurrected itself as a Bavarian Alps village in the 1960s and been a tourist mecca ever since. The kitsch was so complete that it was almost believable. She wondered if even Bavaria looked this German.

Coming east from the fire station, just a block off Route 2—the second biggest east-west highway across the Washington Cascades—she walked right into the heart of "old town." A gazebo on the village green. Red brick cobblestone paving with ornate black cast-iron streetlights. White buildings with that zig-zag dark wood accenting. Generous balconies that dripped with massive red geraniums.

Every building that didn't boast a beer garden was lush with souvenirs. There was a lederhosen store for crying out loud and, she'd seen in the few breaks they'd had from training, that it did a serious business. Tourist kids tromped around town with an ice cream cone and wearing attire right out of *The Sound of Music*.

The only thing open at this hour was the Bavarian Bakery. She was missing breakfast, eggs and bacon no doubt, most of them taking white toast. Why was it that hotshots had no imagination about food? They certainly had to eat enough calories to survive a fire season, but they always went for the fastest and the easiest.

As she walked by the bakery's window, someone slid a tray of delicacies into the display. When the baker saw her hesitation, he flashed her a big smile and waved her to come inside.

The tray looked fantastic.

2

———

Sam Parker waved at her again.

The woman watched him for a long moment, then shrugged and turned for the door.

"First customer and not a tourist. For that you get an extra special treat," he greeted her before the bell even stopped jangling. Not a local either. He'd only bought the bakery a month ago, but there was something in the way she moved that was different.

A tourist rubber-necked and wandered, and if they were up at this hour of the morning then they'd be wearing their runner's togs. Seattle folks who didn't know how to slow down for even one second.

A local would be moving with purpose and direction. This woman had been out strolling at sunrise for the sake of strolling.

"Smells good," she'd stopped one step inside and sampled the air. Most went straight to the big display cases brimming with confectionary. Or headed straight for the register to order their triple-shot skim macchiato, which wasn't a macchiato at all.

Instead she remained where she was long enough to let him really get an eyeful. Her honey-blond hair was short-cropped, and offset her dark eyes. Her face was thin and well-tanned though it was still more late spring than summer.

She wore a yellow shirt and cargo pants with big thigh pockets and serious boots. He could see the power of her despite the loose clothing just in the way she stood.

"I give up." Nobody back in Providence, Rhode Island had ever come into his shop looking like this. He couldn't make sense of her outfit.

She slanted a look over at him, but didn't say a word.

"What are you?"

She raised an eyebrow.

Okay, maybe not the best greeting, so he waved a hand at her attire rather than risking more words. He ran a bakery, words were almost as important as sugar to making a success of it, but he didn't know which words to use with this woman.

She inspected herself carefully and then looked back at him, again raising that single eyebrow. Without the least hint of a smile, she answered, "*Homo sapiens*, female of the species."

At Sam's burst of laughter, she barely blinked.

3

While he laughed, Patsy turned back to inspect the display cases. Most bakeries smelled of sugar, sugar, coffee, and more sugar. But just as a wildfire had hints of cedar, redwood, pine, maple, and a hundred other clues, the air of the Bavarian Bakery was deeply nuanced.

The sugar was there. And the chocolate. But she could smell the butter in the croissants, the apricot in the Danish before she spotted it, the smoothness of rich Bavarian cream, the sharp cinnamon in the baked apple strudel. Hotshots were always lean, there was simply no way to consume more calories than you burned during a season; often there simply wasn't time to do so. But this was a place a woman just might have to be careful. It all looked as incredible as it smelled.

The baker hadn't gone back behind the counter, but instead had remained out front with her. She knew what he'd meant of course, had received the question so many times over the years that the straight answer had long since worn out any interest for her.

A hotshot? What's that?

I fight wildland fires.

Forest fires? Like a smokejumper?

Yes, but without the parachute.

I thought that was a guy thing, jumping out of planes.

As if she hadn't just said…

Sure, hotshots were predominately male. The upper body strength required meant a woman had to want it twice as badly as any man to make the grade—had to bust her ass to overcome genetic predisposition.

Not as unusual as it once was.

It was common now for a hotshot crew to have at least a couple women. The even more strenuous smokejumper roles were starting to see women on the crews as well.

She'd grown so tired of all the stupid follow-on questions, that she'd stopped answering the first one. But usually the men knew she was avoiding a straight answer, grew offended, and left her alone.

This one had laughed, a good laugh. It made her glance back over when she didn't intend to. He didn't look like a German baker: round-faced, blond-haired, and all of the other stereotypes in her brain. He was as lean as she was, an inch or so taller, and his big hands and powerful arms showed a hundred small burn scars and a few older ones that weren't so small. Working with fire. She knew how that looked; had her own fair share of them.

"*Homo sapiens,* male of the species," he answered her apprising look.

She could feel a smile tugging up one corner of her mouth. The man had a sense of humor, and he worked with heat. Even if it was in another form, it was intriguing in its own way.

4

Sam pushed himself up the trail. He'd left the bakery at noon, after a typical nine-hour day, baker's hours. And he enjoyed unwinding on the hiking routes that abounded so close to Leavenworth that he could walk to the trailheads. In Rhode Island, the biggest hill had been eight hundred feet and been a half-hour drive away. Now he lived at twelve hundred feet and couldn't turn around without seeing a half dozen eight thousand footers.

During his one month here, he'd learned that hiking the Cascades was a different challenge than back East, and not just the elevation. A wrong turn there could lead you back to the highway miles away from your car; do the same thing here and you could walk a hundred miles without ever seeing another human, or a road. Wilderness that even jets took a while to cross over. Lost on foot? Very bad news.

Today, he headed off across the flats to the south of town. He'd spotted a plume of smoke up on the hills and used it as an excuse to hike in a new direction. A boxy truck was parked at the base of the trail. Light green with shining golden script, *Cascade Hotshots*.

It was an odd vehicle. The back was a short box with four windows down the sides, like a bus that had its back end sawed off. But instead of being on a bus frame, it was on a very heavy duty truck form, like a cement delivery truck—robust enough to tackle serious loads. Or, he noted that it was parked well across the fields from the nearest street, to negotiate rough terrain. The ride did not look comfortable.

He continued up the trail, the breeze and sun at his back as he climbed. The trail became steep and tough, but he'd learned, and now wore solid boots rather than light walking shoes.

Sam rapidly ascended above the meadow line into the wooded hills, and thought of the woman from this morning.

"Funny how someone can stick in your mind," he told a nodding bush, pulling out his guide long enough to identify it as a huckleberry. He'd have to come back and pick some once they were ripe. He often talked to himself, or at least to the surrounding wildlife as he hiked.

And though he didn't want to be noticing a woman, any woman, she really had stuck in his head. Christi had left him with a gaping wound after a brutal divorce that had sent him all the way to this remote mountain village seeking a bolt hole. Last thing he wanted was to be noticing a woman.

But when he'd watched her eyes flutter shut in appreciation as she bit into his apricot almond bear claw...

Then snap open when her pager buzzed loudly. A quick glance at the small device on her waist and she completely changed.

The slow-moving, slow-smiling woman evaporated as

if she'd never been. Now she was pure business. She folded the bear claw in half and stuffed one end of it into her mouth but didn't bite it off. With her hands free, she dug out her wallet, tossed him a ten dollar bill, and bolted out the door without either her hot chocolate or her change. Maybe she was an ambulance EMT or something. Whatever, she'd simply evaporated.

"Maybe that's what was so intriguing," a chipmunk looked at him doubtfully from its hesitant perch atop a boulder. "My woman of mystery."

The chipmunk laughed and scooted.

So much for that idea.

He rounded a bluff and stumbled to a halt.

He'd been hiking steadily upward through thick conifer forest. His East coast brain would call it a pine forest, but his assistant at the bakery informed him that it was mostly fir trees out here. He'd rounded a boulder in the trail, and the world changed. Before him lay a scene from Dante's *Inferno* so jarring that the transition made little sense.

The low grasses and tall trees were gone, replaced by black char. The trees up ahead were tangled with fire. Flames circled and swirled up the tall trunks, heaving ash into the dark cloud of smoke overhead. A gust sent a spray of embers aloft that danced like fireflies against the black smoke and shining flame before reluctantly winking out. It was beautiful and horrible at the same time.

He looked back over his shoulder. Sun-dappled forest.

He turned ahead once more…

There were figures moving about the base of the flames, people in yellow hardhats and coats.

The souls of the damned!

Another shower of sparks swirled aloft.

It was Hell!

5

atsy worked down the line, checking in with her half of the crew—she and Jess each had nine crewmembers. For their first fire, they were doing well; not that it was a big one. It made for a perfect introduction.

The fire had climbed into a dead-end ravine. Candace had sent scouts both to left and right in case it tried to jump over to the neighboring ravines, but it wasn't big enough to make the leap—again, just good training. They'd think to go themselves next time after checking in with her on the radio. The fire already was dying against the walls and the only ones who didn't know it were the rooks.

The rookies saw the old hands remain calm around them—she'd alternated them down the line so that the rooks couldn't feed off each others' fear—and they had stayed calm in turn. Now it was just a matter of letting it burn out the available fuel in this narrow slot.

She broke out three rooks and a three-year veteran and led them back down to the base of the fire.

"Get a one-and-a-half inch hose into that stream over

there. Start working this line. We don't want to leave a single hotspot. When this is done burning out in a couple hours, we want to have the mop-up mostly finished or we'll miss pizza back in town."

That got them moving. Nothing like the promise of real food and a place to brag about your first fire to motivate a hotshot.

A lone figure with wholly insufficient hiking gear stood at the base of the "black," as the charred area of a wildland forest fire was called, looking like he'd been electrocuted standing up. She considered climbing down to him, but decided to make him hike his pretty, clean gear up through the base of the black and save her the walk. It would stain up his boots and socks pretty good. Then maybe she'd rid herself of yet another gawker to worry about during future blazes.

She waved him up the hill to her.

He hesitated, unsure of himself until she signaled again.

As he approached, she recognized the face from somewhere. Oh, his eyes going wide as she stuffed his delicate pastry into her mouth like a some squirrel stuffing its face full of acorns.

She sighed. Graceful had never been one of her strengths.

---

6

*S*am was only a few paces from the firefighter before he realized it was a woman. The charcoal smeared shirt might have once been yellow. Close-fitting sunglasses hid her eyes. Her hardhat was blue…and smeared black. The rest of the crew's were yellow.

"Why is your helmet a different color?"

The way she tipped her head when she looked at him seemed familiar, and then an eyebrow arched between her sunglasses and helmet.

"Female of the species…" came out half statement and half gasp. It was his woman from the bakery this morning. Firefighter. Wilderness firefighter.

He also recognized the half smile that tugged at her left cheek as she acknowledged him.

"Helmet is blue because I'm a foreman."

"*Foreman?* Wouldn't that be the male of the species?"

"Assistant superintendent if you prefer. The superintendent is the one over there under a hot pink helm. Also a female of the species, though she's taken." He had little more than the impression of someone moving quickly *toward* the inferno until he lost sight of her in the smoke.

Then he glanced once more at her. *She's taken* implied that the woman he was talking to wasn't, and had made a point of it. He was about to ask, but he saw the look of chagrin at her own statement, so he went for a subject change.

"Shouldn't there be helicopters and smokejumpers here?"

She glanced over her shoulder and shrugged, "It's just a baby. I wouldn't want it getting an over-inflated sense of importance. We probably wouldn't even be on it except it's a good training opportunity for a new crew."

If this was a baby, he was completely out of his league. His knees felt loose, so he sat down on a handy rise in the ground. It felt warm through his pants. Even..Hot! He jumped to his feet and brushed hastily at his butt; his hand came away black.

That smile was pulling up the side of her mouth once more.

"Okay, don't play with fire. Got the idea." The ground looked burned and black here just like anywhere else in the vicinity. He reached down to touch the ground by his boots. It felt cool by comparison.

She didn't look so amused anymore.

The woman eased him back a step and then moved forward and kicked the spot where he'd sat. A small flame burped up and was gone.

Sam swallowed against a dry throat.

She was signaling her people to come over, "Okay. See this spot?"

Her crew nodded and studied it.

She waved them back a step and used the flat hoe-like

blade on the back of her fire axe to drag a gouge in it. Flames leapt upward taller than she was.

"That's what you're looking for during mop-up. Doesn't look like much, but they can be a real pain when they reignite, especially if they're behind you. Now, give me some water from the hose."

One of the people had a hose the size of their wrist that trailed back toward the stream.

As she dug into the mound, flames leapt, water shot in, steam erupted.

Sam backed off slowly, finally turned back downslope and headed away. But he kept looking back at the woman casually mopping up a fire, as fearsome as a witch on Hecate's Heath stirring her caldron.

A world of fire and steam he'd never imagined.

atsy hadn't meant to ignore the man, hadn't meant to be rude, but he'd been gone before she finished the training opportunity. And fire always took precedence. They'd done well and were, indeed, back down off the mountain in time for pizza and a beer.

Candace had led them to Maxine's Pizza, a hole in the wall that had no hint of Bavarian from the outside. The insides only confirmed this was a strictly locals' joint. No waitresses in cute Bavarian skirts, no pomp and oom-pah-pah from the jukebox; the Stones were rocking it over the speakers. She went up to the faded "Order Here" sign, and saw that the options were slices or a whole pie and a pint or a pitcher. No burgers, no soups or salads, just pizza that smelled incredible. Worked for her.

Twenty hotshots, first day on the fireline, she ordered eight large pizzas but only three pitchers—they were big here. Maxine returned her change with a smile.

"One beer each, maximum," she told the team. "You never know what tomorrow has for us." She took a diet

Coke and a slice of pepperoni to wait for the pizzas to come up.

Patsy was looking for the logistics needed to pull a bunch of tables together in the crowded dining room when she spotted him. She threaded her way through the noisy area, dodged aside before one of Jess' crew took her out with the back end of a pool cue, and made it to the small table close by the stairs to the upper dining area no worse for the wear.

"May I?" He was reading something in German. Might have been a cookbook.

He blinked up at her in surprise, "Female of the species."

"Patsy Jurgen."

He said something in German that her grandmother might have understood, but was meaningless to her.

"I speak English, bad English, and worse Spanish." It wasn't that her Spanish wasn't fluent enough, it was that while she'd started her education in that language during high school, she'd finished it on the fire line. Vulgar would be putting it politely.

"Oh, sorry. Sam Parker."

"Nope!" she told him as she sat and took a bite out of her pepperoni slice, which really was as good as it smelled.

"What do you mean, *nope?*"

"You read and speak German, and you bake the best apple-cinnamon bear claw I've ever tasted. Does that sound like a Sam Parker to you?"

"Can't say that it does," he sipped a beer. "However, Patricia Jürgen," he said it with a thick German accent, "sounds like a wildland firefighter."

"Thanks, I think. By the way, only Grandma ever called me Patricia." Conversations with attractive men often stumped her, but this one with Sam Parker…

"So, that was really a 'baby' fire?" he waved in exactly the right compass direction indicating a good sense of where he was both indoors and out. He had strong arms, looked very fit; give her a month and she could make him a damn fine firefighter.

"Good for training. This crew was only formed up five weeks ago and the season is just starting up here. Arizona is the one being hammered right now. New Mexico and Colorado will be next. Nevada and Utah don't really have enough to burn. But that's only general patterns. We could light up tomorrow. Normally we would have let the locals deal with something the size of this morning's fire, maybe send a couple of guys to assist."

He looked right and left. Looked down at his beer for a moment.

Patsy had seen this reaction before. Despite Candace's falling for a guy on her crew, that had never been her style. The problem was that someone who wasn't a firefighter never knew what to do with a woman who was.

"So you fight wildfires?"

Why did they always state the obvious before the brush-off. She nodded. Here it came.

Patsy got her feet under her so she could stand and go back to her crew. There, at least, she fit in.

Then Sam grinned at her, "Did I mention that I'm a baker? That's pretty dangerous work you know. Leave out the baking soda and you can be in a world of hurt."

In general Patsy didn't laugh much, but Sam made it easy to join in.

Sam wasn't quite sure how it had happened.

"Sleep deprivation, gotta be," he told the cold strudel dough he'd put in the fridge yesterday, and now pulled out onto the marble slab.

"Up way past my bedtime," he mentioned to the ovens as he lit them off so that they'd be ready for today's bake as soon as he was.

"Damn but that was a hell of a kiss," he told no one and nothing in particular.

Sam usually hit the sack at seven or eight at night and was up and in the kitchen by three at the latest. It was four now and he was behind.

Last night at eight o'clock he'd been watching Patsy risk her life as she went to snag several pieces of pizza from the ravenous group at the hotshots' table. He noted that she picked them up easily though they were still oven hot, usually a trick that only a baker could do. That she returned from her raid unmaimed by the hoard made her all the more impressive.

They'd spent most of the evening bumping knees at his

small table and discovering quite how different two people's pasts could be. Even her mom had been in the fire business; the fire house clerk who had married the captain. Both her brothers rode city engines—he noted the slight scoff in her voice—in Seattle and Boise.

He'd never been to Montana, or was it Idaho. Idaho he decided during his second beer around ten at night. He was the only son of a Boston lawyer and a socialite mother who had married into a prominent Rhode Island family, and then gone to court to get out of it much to his mother's dismay.

They spent most of the evening laughing together. By eleven p.m. and his third beer, it was harder to stop laughing that to start. He noticed she nursed only one glass through the night, but in the laughter department she'd kept right up.

Maxine's Pizza was closer to the fire hall than his small apartment above the bakery. So, he'd walked her through the chill night air, cold enough in June to see his breath despite the lack of streetlights. They were few and far between off the main tourist strips. Whether the city fathers were being cheap or maybe they were trying to encourage tourists to stay in their part of town so that the locals could have some peace and quiet; he wasn't sure which yet. He suspected the latter.

The nearest light had been a block away when they reached her door.

He'd considered saying some cliché about enjoying the evening.

Then he'd considered a different cliché about she was welcome in his bakery any time.

Then he'd kissed her and she'd met him halfway.

It wasn't even a first date, and he'd known her name for only three hours. But he had wanted to discover the taste of her. And though he could still scent the day's fire in her fresh-washed hair, he'd tasted the merriness of her kiss. It was as neatly hidden beneath her serious exterior as the hotspot had been beneath the char this afternoon.

It hadn't started as a friendly little kiss and it certainly hadn't ended like one. They had shared a mutual hum of pleasure before it was done.

"Good night, female of the species."

"Sleep tight, not Sam Parker."

He hadn't noticed the cold at all last night on the five-block walk home from the hotshot's barracks front door—which might have been closer to ten by the time he and his third beer were done with it at midnight. He'd been feeling very mellow and a little lost, in several ways.

For one thing, his ex-wife had left him pretty well convinced that no woman would ever want him. He'd convinced himself that he'd never again risk being with a woman. Yet he'd been here less than two months and just kissed one.

Last night. Just over that way. He glanced in the direction of the hotshot barracks and saw his walk-in refrigerator.

The three a.m. alarm had been a shocker, but he soon lost himself in the dough and date filling, the flavor and texture, trying not to think about how much he'd like to kiss her again.

$\mathcal{P}$atsy was unsure if she was disappointed that the fire season was off to such a slow start, or pleased that it allowed her to pursue her new morning ritual.

That second morning, returning to the bakery, had caused her to hesitate. She didn't hesitate around men, but Sam Parker's kiss the night before had been as sweet as his confections and as powerful as his flavors. It was the power of him that had surprised her, baker's arms and hands meant something, as much strength as a firefighter.

Like a good hotshot, she'd forged ahead through the door and Sam had put her at ease with his immediate smile.

Their initial greeting had been interrupted by an early jogger wanting their coffee fix.

His invitation to come to the back door the next morning had her climbing out of her bunk while the night still ruled the valley and the stars burned above.

A morning kiss, a tall hot chocolate, and the first baked

good out of the oven all served on a flour-dusted counter, while she perched on a high kitchen stool was an excellent way to start the day. He was smart, funny, and enjoyed hiking. She loved his childhood memories as he prepped and baked. Day after day she'd leave him at sunrise to roust the team.

During the evenings, rather than joining the other hotshots, they would wander around town together, as if they couldn't get enough of each other. Trying out different restaurants from waffles to schnitzel. Sometimes they'd go for hikes through the lower hills in the softness of the late light once the sun had plunged beyond the tall peaks to the west. Other times they poked through the souvenir shops, marveling at the things that tourists seemed so eager to own.

There was even a year-round Christmas store right on the main square that was unbelievable. Towering trees, so thick with ornaments and lights for sale that the fake needles were barely visible except as a green backdrop. Vast Christmas villages of tiny ceramic buildings and figurines, even a miniscule skating pond with skaters. It soon became their favorite shop, as there were always new layers to discover. They would meet there before heading off to find a new place to eat. A town of two thousand people and two million tourists boasted an incredible variety of food.

Last night they had visited the animal ornaments display corner of the store and later shared a surprisingly authentic Mexican fajita. Their goodnight kiss had been the third and best element of the evening, parting at sunset as she'd adapted to his hours.

This morning Patsy had woken very early and was at the back door waiting for him when he wandered down the stairs from the apartment above the bakery.

He looked warm and sleepy and rumpled—irresistibly delicious. So she didn't resist.

Sam awoke quickly enough at her welcoming kiss in the kitchen. There was a need that had been building in her over these last weeks, gathering heat and starting to burn.

"I want to take you upstairs," he whispered against her neck.

"I want you to take me right here."

And he did. She wasn't sure what had inspired her to slip some protection in her pocket that morning, but she was glad she had. With her back against the warming ovens, his heat filling her until it felt as if she was burning as brightly as a flame-wreathed tree. His powerful hands were not gentle, but neither were hers. After they'd initially sated their bodies in a fast, bright flare, he moved his mouth over her. As he did, he tasted and tested like she was a fine treat until she climbed once more over the delicious peak and long slow waves of heat rolled over her.

He was late to start his baking that morning, but neither of them was complaining.

It was their first real call up of the season and it was a hot one. Patsy's pager went off just as she was leaving the bakery feeling particularly loose and pleased with herself—and with Sam Parker.

A quick jog to the fire station and she'd found the whole crew loading up into The Box. Patsy made sure that all the gear was stowed properly from yesterday's trail-clearing work and climbed aboard with her team.

Three hours of jostling around in the back of the heavy truck later, they arrived at the base of Mt. Rainer National Park and looked up. The glacier-topped dome of the mountain was a shining beacon of light as the mid-morning sun glittered off the snow.

The fire wasn't on the mountain, but rather on the neighboring Silver King Peak. The fire had at least six heads, probably from multiple lightning strikes, that had already joined into a burn of a thousand acres. They couldn't just let it burn, because if it climbed up and over the mountain, it would take out the Crystal Mountain Ski Resort, the largest one in the state.

The primary approaches were already engulfed in the fire.

Patsy had been gearing up for the long hike in, seething with frustration at how long it would take them to get to the fire going over rough country on foot. There were no roads for The Box, not even bad ones.

Candace took one look at the situation and pulled out her radio.

"Incident Commander. This is Cascade Hotshots requesting helitack."

Of course. That's why she was the boss. Candace rocked.

Minutes later a pair of big, black-and-flame painted Firehawk helicopters from Mount Hood Aviation descended through the smoky sky and landed in the same clearing as The Box.

A man jumped down and moved past the rotors quickly, pausing just a moment to snap their photo. He looked like a goof with the two cameras—a handsome goof—but he walked like a hotshot. MHA was a top outfit, maybe he was both.

"Hi, name's Cal. Ten of you with Jeannie and me, ten with Emily," he waved at the other helicopter. "Rugged terrain up there, so you're going in by rope."

"Harness up," she shouted to the team. As soon as she had hers on, she checked her team, pleased with how little she found to correct.

Now, they were soaring aloft, packed in the back of the Firehawks like firewood, and Candace asked her, "Who is he?"

"I—" Patsy closed her mouth, unsure what to say.

"Oh, yeah. I recognize that look," Candace shouted over the helicopter's roar.

Patsy studied her boss' face, but couldn't read what was there.

"Same thing happened with Luke. There I was, going along ever so happily, and then snap!" she made a twig breaking motion. "The whole world changed."

Patsy didn't know about the whole world, but certainly a portion of it had.

She surveyed the fire as they climbed skyward alongside the steep ridges, looked at how it was moving along the hills.

Patsy pointed and Candace nodded, their first point of attack was obvious from this height—a few hundred meters from the north flank of the fire; keep it from going any wider here. Candace leaned forward between the seats to tell the pilot.

The other thing that Patsy could see was that she wasn't going to be back in time for dinner, perhaps not for days.

She pulled out her cell phone, probably no reception once they hit the ground out here in the National Park, and certainly no time. She caught two bars off a tower somewhere and dialed Sam's number.

Patsy had never had anyone to call before, when going to a fire. She'd simply go, for a day, a week, a month; it didn't matter. Once a week she tried to let Mom and Dad know she was alive, but they understood if she didn't check in during a busy fire season. They'd taught her to be safe around fire by the time she entered kindergarten. And how to fight it while still in middle school.

She got Sam's answering machine.

"Hey, this is Patsy. I'm off on a fire. Will let you know when I'm back." She didn't know what else to say. Nothing appropriate except how much she'd enjoyed having sex in his kitchen this morning. And meeting him in the evenings.

And eating his delicious creations. "Uh, thanks," was the best, lame-ass thing she came up with.

Patsy hung up the phone and tucked it away as the helicopter circled down on their chosen position.

She'd be the first one down, so she clipped her rappelling harness onto the line tied off to the loop outside the cargo bay door.

Candace was back beside her and double-checked Patsy's gear.

"He's a baker," Patsy told her. Which explained absolutely nothing about him.

The helicopter was sliding to a halt just above the treetops. Patsy tossed the coiled line out the cargo bay door and watched as it snaked down and disappeared through a narrow gap in the trees.

Candace's bland look told her that wasn't nearly enough explanation.

"He's really good with his hands."

At that Candace smiled and nodded enthusiastically, "Don't you just love men with good hands?"

Patsy leaned forward out of the cargo bay, then she slid down beneath the battering wind of the rotor, the fire's radiant heat powerful on her face even at this distance.

Heat. A man who worked with heat and generated it as well with those nice hands of his.

Love? She wasn't there yet, but for the first time in her life she could imagine getting there. Much the same way she could imagine beating this fire, though they hadn't even begun.

She hit the ground and disengaged from the line, but her feet were still floating somewhere up in the sky.

11

Six days.

Sam was amazed at how many emotions had churned up within him in six days.

First, disappointment that Patsy was gone and he didn't have an immediate opportunity to test if what had been between them that morning was real…or even repeatable.

This near stranger, naked and unabashed in his kitchen, had been a revelation. His first time with her had been better than any time with Christie—and throughout their marriage they'd both always remarked on how good they were together physically. Until she was also good, and unrepentant, with her married boss.

Patsy had been incredible, responding in ways he'd never imagined. And where Christie had been delicate, cultivating it into a fine, fragile art form, Patsy was powerful. She definitely gave back as good as she got, and she was impossibly, fantastically real. He'd also had no idea how amazing the body of a "female of the species" could form up until he'd had a chance to appreciate Patsy Jurgen's immense degree of fitness.

Besides, she wasn't a stranger. In their evenings together, he'd found it easy to spill out tales of his past. At first he avoided his marriage, divorce, and abandoning his job. But that too eventually came out in the comfortable world they'd created between them.

"I always wanted to own my own bakery instead of cooking in someone else's. That was about the only good thing I got out of the whole mess."

It was only after he'd said the words that he thought of how they might have sounded to this woman he was now seeing. They certainly wouldn't have met if not for his moving across the whole country to get away from Christie.

But Patsy hadn't taken some unintended offense. Instead, she'd remarked that if his business sense was as good as his food sense, he was set for life. It was good, but he'd signed up for an on-line business course that night to make sure of it.

She was more reticent than he was, but once she started a tale, she told it without any attempt to evade or be embarrassed by it. She told the good with the bad as if the past was of no consequence at all.

He worried less about the past the more time they spent together.

What he hadn't expected was to, once more, start looking forward to the future. That was a skill Christie had taken in the divorce that he was only now rediscovering.

He went through disappointment that he didn't hear from Patsy. Then anger. Surely the woman could find the damned time to text the man she'd just had sex with. Maybe that's all she'd wanted, one good screw, and was now done with him. He knew that was wrong about her, but it didn't stop it from swirling through his mind like folding a meringue time and again until it was totally flat and useless—an immensely frustrating twenty-four hours.

When he still didn't hear from her, he shifted over to fear that she'd been injured or killed and no one would know to tell him.

After two nights in a row of lost sleep, he went down to the Leavenworth fire station for lack of any better idea.

Captain Carl Cantrell was in his office.

Patsy had talked a lot, for her, about Candace Cantrell —the fire chief's daughter and head of the Cascade Hotshots. Practically worshipped the ground the woman walked on.

"Patsy?" Cantrell had offered him an easy smile. "She's still off on the Silver King Fire. Just heard from my girl last night on the radio. She thinks they'll have it contained in another day, two max. Once they can hand it off to a Type 2 mop-up crew, they'll be back, unless there's another blow-up."

On the radio. Not somewhere she could call, which could explain why Patsy hadn't called. No phone service.

Type 2? Not a clue.

At least he knew what "mop-up" looked like, columns of fire erupting from ground that pretended to be black and dead.

Blow-up he definitely didn't like the sound of.

"You the one put that smile on her face?"

Sam was tempted to avoid answering, but could feel the smile of relief on his own, knowing she was fine, just out doing her job.

"I hope that's because of me."

Cantrell just kept grinning, "Keep it up, son. That smile looks good on her. She takes it all far too seriously."

"Well, she fights fires for a living," he felt himself getting deeply protective of her.

The man held up his hands in a placating motion. "Do some of that myself."

Right, this is the Fire Chief, you dolt.

"She's a good one and I've seen enough to know. Maybe as good as my Candace, though if you say in front of my daughter I'll deny it. Just needs someone to lighten her up a bit."

Deeply comforted by the news and the Captain's words, Sam headed back into town to wait. He wanted to get her something. Something to tell her that he thought she was incredible.

As he passed the Christmas shop, he knew just what to get.

1 2

---

*B*ack in town Patsy crawled out of The Box and into the shower. Eight days on the first fire of the season. She'd slept…hmm, she was sure she'd slept at some point. They'd *coyoted* for much of the fire, lying down in their gear right where they finished a shift—usually twenty-four to thirty-six hours long—and slept until the fire made an aggressive move and you were on your feet again—usually way too soon.

She plunged into her first shower in all that time and let the stink wash down the drain with the char. Clothes in the wash.

She came to, standing upright and staring down at her bunk. Yes, she should just do a faceplant and hope nothing burned in the next twenty-four hours. But she didn't want to.

Instead, she was halfway to town before she knew what she wanted. Her brain was definitely moving slower than her body.

Eight days.

All Sam Parker had gotten from her in eight days was

63

silence. Would he still want to see her? She thought so. She hoped so.

It was amazing how much he'd been in her head through all that time.

Instead of just living the moment of the fire, she wanted to tell him about it. The little victories, the staggering defeats, and the return to battle until it was won. There was no option, winning is what hotshots did, engaging the fire until it was down and done.

She didn't think that Sam would need a bribe in order to want her back. But she wanted to take him something to let him know she'd been thinking of him.

*S*am had decided to hang out late in the bakery that day even though his assistants had it covered. Late morning he'd gotten a call from the Fire Chief.

"They're home. Doesn't look like they've slept much, probably shower and sack time, but I thought you'd want to know."

He left the back door open as he worked in the kitchen. It was after lunch when a shadow cut the light pouring into the kitchen, even as he made some notes to try next time on the banana muffins.

He turned to see her, for he had no doubt it would be Patsy. Something inside him just knew.

She stood there, framed in the sunlit doorway. Instead of her fire gear, she wore shorts and sneakers that revealed those powerful legs that had been clamped so tight around his waist that one morning.

Her t-shirt was bright red with a jagged yellow line like mountain peaks, but also like fire. Block letters spelled out, "Silver King Fire" and the year. It hugged her curves in ways that just begged for him to explore them.

Her golden hair caught the sunlight like a halo of fire.

"I got you something," she held up a small bag that he recognized.

Sam reached under the counter and pulled out a similar bag, "I know it's only June, but it just seemed right."

He actually felt awkward as they exchanged bags; it was a surprisingly intimate moment. They began to open them together on the steel prep table.

He pulled out a string of lights and couldn't help smiling. It was a totally ridiculous string of tiny baked goods: cakes, éclairs, and cookies.

Sam waited while she finished upwrapping her own set of "Fiery Twinkle Lights." He snagged the plug and put it into the outlet under the lip of the counter, then he plugged in his string to hers. Together they all flashed on and hers began to flicker like fire.

"They look good together," her voice was soft, on the verge of that rare laugh he'd so come to enjoy.

"They do," he agreed. Then he looked up at her, "You look incredible."

"So do you," she took a step closer and nodded toward the steel prep table, the reflection doubling the lights. "It looks like between us we have a good start on a Christmas tree."

"A very good beginning," Sam moved in a step, could feel the warmth of Patsy Junger's heat spreading through him as that lopsided smile of hers broke free.

"I bet that between us, we could make an incredible tree by December." She slid into his arms and wrapped her own arms around his back. She rested her head against his shoulder.

"I'm sure you're right."

And she was.

There had never been a gift so perfect as this woman in his arms.

FIRE LIGHT CABIN BRIGHT

Hotshot Tori Ellison *loves fighting wildfire. Her passion runs so deep that her firefighter nickname "Ginger" came from her team leader's never-say-enough ball-chasing Labrador.*

__Colin James__ chose his mountain cabin hideaway to write his next novel and recover from his ex-wife. When Tori lands face first in his vegetable garden to warn him of an approaching wildfire, a whole new chapter opens before them.

Now if they can just avoid getting burned in the Fire Light Cabin Bright.

INTRODUCTION

Being on an Interagency Hotshot Crew is brutally tough. These teams, twenty in a pack, ride in a small truck called a "Box." It is tightly cramped with gear and firefighters, and it is also the very core of their operation. The Box delivers these teams as close as they can to a wildfire, then they load up with heavy gear and tools (often fifty to seventy pounds worth), and *walk* to the fire—typically miles over horrendous terrain to even reach the firefight. Once there, the battle against the fire is a hand-waged war that allows few breaks and even less sleep.

For five to seven months every summer, they battle fire with only very rare days off. Their pay is unimpressive (off season many make the ends meet working as bartenders or ski patrol at winter resorts), but their drive is powerful and heartfelt. These are people who love the wilderness and the firefight and give it all they have—it is also far too dangerous to give it less. They are often literally toe-to-toe with the fire.

There are some women now qualifying in these positions and proving that they have what it takes. These are strong, powerful women with a bloody-minded level of perseverance when it comes to fighting fire.

For people who like the obscure connections that I sometimes build into my stories, Tori is inspired to fight fire by a brief fling with the smokejumper Akbar the Great in Firehawks book #1 *Pure Heat.*

Tori is also an homage to a college friend. Whenever I think of someone who knew no fear of trying something new, it was her. When cancer took her only a decade later, it was like a light had gone out in the world. I wanted to give her the future she deserved but never had time to find.

And when I was trying to think of who Tori would be running up against in this romance, I wanted someone as opposite from her as I could find. So I chose a writer…and wished him luck.

Thankfully, it turned out that he had some ideas of his own to surprise Tori.

1

____

Just as some days are hotter than others, some fires are hotter than others. And the Checker Mill Fire was a scorcher.

Tori Ellison checked her watch but couldn't see it. Even shining her helmet headlamp on it didn't really help. Her eyes were lack-of-sleep sore and they stung from smoke and salty sweat. She couldn't taste anything but that salt and the char that it collected as it dribbled down her face; the peanut and dark chocolate flavor of her energy bar hadn't lasted more than a few minutes before being overwhelmed.

She'd volunteered to scout what lay over the next ridge while the rest of her Hotshot fire crew crashed out for an hour. She was supposed to go ten minutes out and ten back, but couldn't seem to focus on the watch to tell how long she'd been gone. Three minutes? Fifteen? She no longer knew.

It was zero-dark-thirty, like the military guys said, which was all that really mattered.

Where was here? She wasn't so sure of that either.

She was always doing dumb, impulsive things like this.

In college one of her nicknames had been the Energizer Bunny because she'd never had the sense to stop until she dropped. The Bunny part had been shed after she'd punched a particularly obnoxious frat boy hard enough to shatter his nose.

When Tori hit the fire line, her new firefighter nickname was Ginger within three days.

It wasn't that her hair was red—she was a bob-cut blond. The crew chief, Candace Cantrell, had grown up with a Labrador named Ginger who also never knew when to stop.

A low-hanging Douglas fir branch slapped in her face because she was too weary to step around it. At least it was green and smelled of life and fresh pine. She felt bolstered by its presence; it was standing in the cool forest night, trusting her and her team to save it from the encroaching wildfire.

Tori trudged by it and promised to do her best— trudged because trotting was long past her abilities at the moment. They'd come off the Bell Creek Fire along Washington's Skagit River less than forty-eight hours ago and now had been on the Checker Mill for the last thirty- six straight. The Cascade Mountains were rough and she normally liked the challenge…when she was conscious.

She crested the low ridge in a thick stand of trees. It would take a lot of cutting to clear a fire line here if they had to. Too tired to even dodge the branches, she raised her arms in front of her face and ploughed through the heart of the stand.

The trees gave way the moment before her feet snarled in thick vines and she face-planted on the ground.

Her radio crackled, "Ginger, check in."

"Yo, Candace." The ground was soft. Well-tilled soil

cool against her cheek. She didn't waste extra effort trying to stand up. It felt so good to lie down, for even a moment.

"Report."

"Hard-ass," Tori teased her. Since it was something the Hotshot team's leader was proud of, it was a safe call. "Trees much thicker at the ridge. Eight to eighteen-inch diameter Doug fir. Can't see much else."

"Where are you now?"

"Lying on the ground," she looked around to try and be more specific, and was confronted by something large and green. Big enough to completely block her view. "In a zucchini patch."

"A residence?"

That would be bad news. Needing to defend a residence, or worse a neighborhood, could drastically change a fire attack plan.

"Ginger?"

"Hang on. Hang on. Sheesh!" Tori forced her arms beneath her and levered herself upward. They shook with the effort. She'd really tapped herself out this time; right out to the limits.

Once upright she twisted her head side to side to swing the headlamp around.

"I'm in a vegetable garden," she reported.

"You're in *my* vegetable garden, 'Ginger'," a deep male voice sounded from the dark.

She twisted the lamp around and found a mountain man standing about ten feet down a row of tomatoes. Except he wasn't hairy, messy, or clad in rotting animal skins. He wore gym shorts and a frown. She couldn't see his eyes because he had his arm raised to protect them from the glare of her lamp, but from the nose down was very fine. Not a six-pack ab guy, but no extra bits either.

"Who are you? And why were you eavesdropping on my private conversation?"

"My name's Colin James. And if you're in my garden on the radio, how private can your conversation be?"

Tori hit the transmit key, "I'm in Colin's secret garden. And he's just as much of a know-it-all as the one in the book."

"If Dickon shows up, he's mine," Candace replied. "I always had a crush on Dickon."

Tori heard a soft *Hey!* in the background, probably Candace's husband Luke, a top member of the IHC crew.

"What are you doing in my squash?" the man asked from behind his raised arm.

"Well, that's no way to address a lady, Colin."

2

Her voice was the only thing that distinguished her as one. Colin had been lying out in the hammock watching the stars—it was too beautiful and warm a night to stay in his cabin—when he'd heard a hard grunt and rustle from his vegetable garden.

It had sounded human rather than ursine—he didn't worry about bears here…much. When he'd looked, there was a light shining low under his plants. Not stopping for shoes or a flashlight, he raced out to scare away the poacher. He'd put a lot of time and care into his garden and no midnight skulker was going to rob him.

He'd been stopped in his tracks by what he found. Between the zucchini and the pumpkins lay a fully clad firefighter, and one that was making no effort to get up.

By the reflected light off the nearby leaves, Colin had seen a hardhat that might have once been yellow under all the soot. The firefighter wore similarly colored jacket and pants, heavy boots, and a small pack. One hand clutched a nasty-looking axe and the other a handheld radio.

And then the firefighter had spoken and turned out to be a she. Named Ginger.

"If you're lying in my vegetables, I'll address you any way I choose. And get that light out of my eyes."

"Oh, sorry," she turned the lamp toward the ground.

He had a brief glimpse of an oval face and a hint of blond hair before she flicked it off and they were plunged into darkness. He blinked hard, but his night vision was shot and wouldn't be back for several minutes.

He couldn't see, but he could hear that she hadn't moved.

"Are you planning to just lie there all night among my veggies?"

She giggled. "You have a very comfortable garden." A firefighter who giggled.

"What are you doing here anyway?"

"Uh," Ginger paused. "I'm here because..." she sounded as if she was trying to figure that out for herself, "...oh, yeah. I'm here because there's a forest fire in the next valley over. I'm the scout."

Suddenly a dozen things he hadn't paid any real attention to earlier in the day made sense. He'd kept smelling wood smoke, but no one in their right mind would have their fireplace going on such a hot day. Besides, he was pretty sure that he had no neighbors for a long way in any direction.

Also there had been clouds to the north, but he hadn't really paid attention. The novel was finally going well and he hadn't been outside all day. Yet another reason he'd retired to the hammock with the sunset. Now though, he remembered that the clouds had been an odd color for a lightning storm, too dark.

There'd also been the sound of helicopters, but they

were often used in logging operations. Maybe not so much today.

"How close?" he swallowed hard.

"A mile or so. I seem to have lost track."

"What kind of a firefighter are you?"

"An exhausted one."

"Here," he reached out into the dark. "Let me help you up."

Somehow they found each other's hands. But when he braced a foot forward to pull her up, he stepped barefoot right on a planting stake. He tumbled forward onto her with an exclamation on his part and a curse on hers.

"That's your idea of being helpful?" she grumbled from where she lay beneath him in the dark.

"Ginger, this is Candace," the radio squawked loudly in his ear. "Are we looking at an individual or a community? I don't show anything on the map."

He tried to roll off her, but the big zucchini bush stopped him. When he shifted the other direction, he partly rolled onto her fireaxe.

"Hey Candace. I can confirm an individual. Clumsy, but cute."

"I'm not—" Well, maybe he was being a klutz. But he hadn't exactly been prepared for a female firefighter lying on the dirt in his garden.

"Ginger!" The woman on the radio was sounding irritated.

"Hang on." Then Ginger reached up to assist him in getting off her, and clipped him fairly solidly on the jaw with a leather-gloved fist.

He tumbled into the vines.

"Oh crap. I'm sorry." She giggled again even as she groped around in the darkness, grabbed his arm for support, which pulled him back atop her with surprising strength. "Well, isn't that interesting."

This time when he tried to pull himself free, she pulled him down and kissed him. Hard.

3

———————

What was she doing? Tori was deep in the kiss before any part of her brain woke up enough to be rational. The mostly unclad Colin was lying full upon her and, after a brief hesitation, was proving he was an exceptional kisser.

After enjoying the situation for several more moments, she managed a "Whoa." Then she pushed against his shoulders to shift him up and far enough away for her head to stop having ideas about where to go next with this mostly naked man. He tasted deliciously of male and toothpaste—a welcome relief from her own salt sweat and char—but it was dumb as could be for her to randomly kiss a total stranger.

Colin didn't resist as she pushed him back. Kept going until he was kneeling between her legs.

"Um," she had nothing to add to that. And she was almost tired enough to drag him back down on her.

"Ginger!"

"Spoilsport," she told the radio without keying the transmit key.

"She's persistent," Colin observed from nearby in the darkness. Her eyes had recovered enough to make out his outline against the stars.

"You have no idea. She needs to know…" something.

"I live alone here. Solo cabin. Is the fire coming my way?"

"Candace," somehow Tori had held onto the radio during the kiss. "It's a solo cabin of a man who tastes like mountain spring water."

"You kissed him?"

"Either I did or he did. I'm a little fuzzy on the details."

"Uh-huh," Candace wasn't buying it. "I'll send Luke up with a couple saws. Make sure the site is prepped for best defense. The fire has slowed and will be good until dawn. We'll get air attack to lay down a perimeter as soon as the helos are back aloft with the sunrise. Take an hour break."

"Roger that."

Now the question was, what to do with an hour?

4

On the gas camping stove, Colin had heated up the leftover chili he'd been planning to have for lunch tomorrow. The woman across the table was wolfing it down while it was still scalding hot as if she hadn't eaten in a week.

"Don't they feed you?"

"Only between fires. No time during a burn. You cook this?" She mumbled around a mouthful, halfway through the bowl.

"Yes, my chef is off this week."

"It's good," she drank back a glass of water in a single gulp. "Really good." She slowed down and began looking around the candlelit cabin. "I see the butler is off this week too."

He looked around and grimaced. "I'm not generally this messy." He was ten miles up a dead-end road and an hour-long hike on a steep trail past that. He hadn't exactly prepared for visitors. And it wasn't that bad. His sheets were still spread on the couch, his clothes piled on the chair, and the floor hadn't been swept in a while. But the dishes were clean and the food all stowed. His desk was a train wreck, but that was always the case when he was in the middle of writing a novel.

At least he'd taken a wash in the stream recently. Colin rubbed at his chin. Okay, should have shaved somewhere in the last few days, but how was he supposed to have known that he was going to have his first-ever visitor in five summers.

"You're not exactly all spic-and-span yourself," he told her.

She'd staggered into his cabin, dumping hardhat, jacket, and axe across the threshold. The cotton shirt she wore underneath was both sweat- and soot-stained. But it clung to her in amazing ways. The easy strength she'd revealed in the vegetable garden was evident in her athlete's shoulders. Her curves were feminine and sleek; as unlike his ex-wife as could be.

Mirella had been voluptuous…and needy as hell. The latter had made him feel the powerful protector at first, but what had started out as charming had become a cloying emptiness in the woman that could never be assuaged. He'd been on the verge of running and damn the expenses, when she'd decided to fill that emptiness with another man. He was still smarting from the whole mess— despite his lucky escape—and was not looking for another woman.

But looking *at* the woman before him was proving to be a pleasure.

"You're staring."

He was. "I am," he shrugged an apology. "You offer a lot to look at, Ginger." Her fitness, her curves, the face that would have looked merely nice on any lesser woman. Ginger's face was alive with emotion; smile or sarcasm, her feelings showed easily past the deep exhaustion.

"That's not my name."

"But on the radio…" he trailed off at her self-deprecating smile.

"Nickname I earned for being as dumb as a dog. Tori Ellison," she held out a hand and he shook it, "I never know when to quit."

"Easy answer, never."

5

————————

ori looked up at Colin sharply. It *was* the easy answer, but no one else ever understood that.

Hotshot crews were trained to keep going no matter what, right until the hallucinations of exhaustion set in, and she was still twenty-four hours from that state. But for everyone else, it was always a challenge to keep going. To push harder.

Instead, Tori always saw it as never having "quit" as an option. It made all the difference in the world, but she'd never been able to explain that to anyone satisfactorily.

"What makes you say that?" she asked carefully as she continued to eat the magnificent chili.

Colin looked around his cabin as if he'd stored the answer to her question somewhere in the room.

It was a sweet setup. A generous one-room; a mountain cabin without being primitive. Big windows that told of a magnificent southern view hidden by the darkness. They sat at a small table for two that might be more workbench than dining table. A hand pump at the sink spoke volumes.

But there were also shelves of books, a cozy wood stove, and, perched at a desk cluttered with paper and books, sat a small laptop computer—the only sign of electricity in the whole cabin. She spotted the large battery and would bet that there was a solar panel somewhere outside that fed it. The laptop, she decided, was the focus of the room. The rest was disorganized, not because he was a slob—for the kitchen was immaculate—but because he didn't care.

He too had turned to the desk as if the answer was there somewhere but he couldn't see it. No. He saw it clearly, but wasn't sure about sharing it.

"Writer's cabin," she guessed.

He nodded, then froze like a animal wondering if it was too late to escape the fire.

"Published."

A very careful nod.

So, not a comfortable topic. Which meant he was either a total failure or a major success. If the former, the kitchen wouldn't be so neat...or the desk so messy; a failure would fail in multiple ways. So, a success that he didn't want to reveal, that had him living in a remote cabin with a vegetable garden.

She returned to her study of him rather than his cabin. Not a burden. Tori had thought he was good-looking by the light of her head lamp, but his arm had hidden his best feature. Warm brown eyes lively with a sharp brain behind them. A writer's brain. But they were also warm with emotion, and each time they drifted down her body, more and more heat was revealed there.

"I dated a writer once," she said without thinking first.

"I hate him already," Colin offered the comment amiably.

"He was okay. But he didn't understand about

perseverance." Tori had learned enough while dating Andy to know that writing was all about perseverance. She could see that Colin was surprised she knew that reality.

"You're frustrating me at the moment," he remarked and it sounded like a topic change, so she let it be.

"Good. Only one thing this girl likes more than frustrating a handsome, successful man."

"What's that?"

And suddenly Tori was the one who wanted the topic change. She knew that she was far too tired if she'd let that slip out. She'd gotten into firefighting courtesy of a brief fling with a smokejumper. He'd been fun enough, but their brief foray into the wilderness had been life changing.

Tori had always like the outdoors. She'd earned dual degrees in botany and ecology before that trip. To hang with a group of firefighters deep in the wilderness had been an option she'd never thought of until she met the smokie in a bar. He'd offered the briefest glimpse of a life in that uncontemplated world of wildland firefighting.

She'd even found it easy to fall in with the typical firefighter talk once she became one. But there was still a woman with a dream who'd been born on that trip.

The smokie's bosses had been along on the trip, a pair of heli-aviation pilots. A man and woman and their little daughter. Neither spoke much, but their unity—their perfect togetherness—had been such a daunting vision, that it had set the bar impossibly high. She wanted what they had.

Candace and Luke were another couple that felt that way—the only other example she'd ever met.

So, she trained and became a hotshot. On the teams she laughed and teased, and occasionally played the "I fight wildfires for a living" card to pick up a handsome man in a bar. But there was a part of her that dreamed of finding that "right man" someday.

That was the thing that this girl wanted more than frustrating a handsome, successful man.

Not a chance she'd be admitting that out loud though.

6

---

olin watched her sleep.

He'd offered the couch, but she didn't want to mess it up with her soot-stained clothes. Instead, she landed in his back-porch hammock and was out in seconds. He parked himself in an Adirondack chair on the back porch and again took in the night.

The stars that he'd been watching to the east, were blocked to the west—the direction Tori had arrived from—by dark clouds. They weren't black, as clouds usually were at night, but glowed red along the bottoms as if they still caught the last of the long-past sunset.

Fire. They glowed red with fire. The hints of wood smoke from this morning were more constant, though still swirled aside by the gentle night breezes. Close, but not too close. Staying far away, he hoped.

He should go inside. Pack his notes and laptop in a bag so that he could grab it and go if he had to. But he couldn't break the easy comfort of sitting and watching Tori sleep.

The charge on his body guaranteed that any chance of

sleep for himself lay a long way off. Pretty, motivated, tenacious, and smart were only a few of the adjectives he cataloged on her behalf. She'd synthesized what he was all about with very few clues, and then had the decency to read that he didn't want to talk about it.

Mirella, despite being the one who'd cheated on him, had wanted a big piece of who he was when she left. She wanted rights to any books he'd written while they were together and any number of other things that his attorney had refused to give up. By the time the acrimonious battle was complete, Colin had paid her nothing and she had convinced him that the only reason she'd ever been with him had been avarice. He liked to think that hadn't been the case. But however it had started, it had nothing to do with love.

He wondered what Tori was like when she wasn't drugged with exhaustion. Still beautiful. Still thoughtful. Still tenacious. He was surprised that he'd very much like to discover more despite swearing off women.

Colin knew too little to make conjectures, but he had enjoyed every waking moment they'd had together, at the table and even lying in the garden's dirt.

That kiss. That brief, spectacular kiss. That had been one thing about Mirella, the sex with her was always fantastic. She might have needed something he couldn't supply to send her seeking another man's bed, but the woman had been built hot and made to last.

He'd kissed Tori for approximately three seconds, and it washed any lingering, lonely-night fantasies of Mirella right out of his mind. If kissing Tori was that good, what would the rest of it be like?

"Been alone in the woods too long," he told the night quietly.

Colin came to the mountain cabin to write. To get

away from people and the city and the distractions. He'd been seriously considering wintering over this year despite the harsh winters that sometimes swept the heights of the Cascades. Mirella had come to the cabin once, and departed rapidly. He'd guess that if he chose to winter over, Tori would be right there with him. And loving it.

He watched over her until a small light came bobbing toward him through the darkness. A tall man wearing a headlamp came up to the porch, flashed his light on Tori's sleeping face and then a quick scan around—without blinding Colin—before dousing the light.

"Name's Luke," the man stepped forward and offered a hand. His shake was strong, firefighter strong.

"Colin."

"She actually looks sweet when she's asleep," Luke commented.

"How about when she's awake?"

"Still sweet," Luke chuckled. "Telling you, something's gotta be wrong with the woman to be so consistently pleasant and cheery, but I haven't found it yet. She's a born firefighter. Thanks for watching over her, not that this one needs it."

"What does she need?"

7

———

ori would have to pay Luke back for the "sweet" wisecrack.

"Don't think it's my place to be giving away any of the lady's secrets," Luke was telling Colin. "Why? You got an interest?"

Tori lay very still and awaited the answer.

"Might."

Colin *might* have an interest? All she'd done was punched him, kissed him…spectacularly, eaten his chili, and passed out in his hammock for an hour. She was about to rouse herself, despite how comfortable she was feeling, and give these two a quick whack with an axe handle just for being so male, when Luke finally replied.

"If you want to find a better person than Victoria Ellison, you're too late; I already married her. My Candace." Then Luke slapped her on the calf. "Rise and shine, Ginger. We've got some trees to trim. You're first up swamping."

Tori made a groan for Luke's benefit. When cutting line, one person was the sawyer, and the other hauled everything they cut as far from the fire line as possible. They'd switch off after every tank of fuel, but going from nice soft hammock to swamping was a rude awakening.

But Luke's compliment was high praise indeed; he was crazy about Candace and deservedly so. She didn't know that Luke thought that highly of her as well.

Luke tramped off toward the trees.

Tori waited a moment by Colin, wishing she could see him better.

"Thanks for taking me in," she didn't know what else to say.

"You're welcome any time," he sounded surprised at this own words.

Whether she was unwilling to risk another supercharged, mega-turbo kiss, or the hour's sleep had been sufficient for her common sense to return, she merely shook his hand and turned for the trees.

He *might* have an interest?

It was stupid. It was based on nothing at all.

The only problem she could think of was that she *might* be having an interest as well.

8

Colin brewed coffee, pulled on boots and work clothes, and headed up the slope to join them. He did pack his grab bag and leave it inside the door just in case.

The coffee was taken, appreciated, and drunk while still too hot.

Tori, who was running the chain saw by the time he arrived, didn't even shut off the saw when she knocked her coffee back like a drug, then returned the mug with the briefest of nods. He almost didn't recognize her in the soft pre-dawn light. For one thing, she was back in her full helmet and gear. But also, she was in Ginger-mode. She was moving full tilt and nothing was going to break her focus. He knew that feeling and did his best not to feel rejected by her lack of acknowledgement.

She had cleats on her boots and a heavy belt that wrapped around the fir. She scaled up the tree to the lowest dead branches, then nipped them off with the saw. Moving the belt higher, the next dead branches dropped to the ground. In moments she was fifty feet in the air and a thick pile of dead branches had accumulated around the base of the tree.

Luke was at the prior tree, gathering up the dead branches and dragging them in the direction of the cabin. Douglas firs grew tall, and the lower branches often died off, yet still hung on for years.

Colin grabbed a bundle of branches and followed Luke. Luke had found the cliff edge below the cabin and dumped the branches over which then tumbled to the bottom. Even if they somehow caught fire there, all they'd do was scorch some rock. Colin pitched his load over and they walked back together.

"I don't get what we're doing."

"Ladder fuels," Luke replied. "Fire wants to burn and climb up a tree. Get rid of undergrowth and it has less to burn, stays cooler on the ground. Cut away the deadwood and it has nothing to climb. The real problem happens when it reaches the crown. Hard to fight a crown fire from the ground."

With two of them swamping, they made quick work of what had already been cut.

Luke fired up a second saw and began clearing the undergrowth. Colin couldn't keep up with both of them, but whenever Tori or Luke ran out of fuel, they'd help him catch up as part of their refueling. Mid-morning he knew trouble was coming when a tanker plane roared by low overhead and dumped a broad swath of retardant on the trees. For a quarter mile, the big jet plane sent down a shower of the dark red liquid in an impossibly dense downpour.

Tori arrived beside him as the tanker finished the run and turned back for its next load. "Retardant coats the wood and keeps the oxygen from reaching it. No oxygen means no fire."

"Then what have we been doing here?" Colin waved at the trees, at the whole area they'd been parking-out.

"Layers of defense, like chapters in a book. Chapter One, we have a fireline cut about a half mile back. We're hoping to narrow the blaze, maybe even knock it out of the crown because it's running high and hot at the moment. Chapter Two, hopefully most of it dies when it hits the retardant line. Chapter Three, if we can really slow it down here, it won't do much more than mow the grass in your meadow before we can extinguish it. End of story."

He'd been right about smart and kind. She'd thought to switch her words into his metaphor to make sure he understood it easily, rather than assuming he could cross to her side of the fence.

"And if all three chapters fail? What's the fourth?" He'd miss his cabin. He'd rebuild, but there were a lot of good memories here; he could hear the stories that had been written in this idyllic spot.

She pointed up at the sky.

A small helicopter painted black with red flames came pounding up the hill. They watched it together as it flew over his cabin, a huge, bright-orange bucket on a cable dangled far below. The pilot didn't even slow down, just released the load of water dead-center on his roof. It soaked down the shingles and poured off the eaves in a waves.

"That's the epilogue, just in case the fire didn't get the message or tries to throw a few hot embers your way."

Colin could see it clearly. All of the different pieces and how they fit together as neatly as any story.

But he couldn't stop looking at the quietly competent woman he'd been working beside all morning.

"Just in case I don't get a chance to say it later, I meant what I said. You're welcome anytime."

9

ori didn't know what she was doing. It was her first break in weeks. The fire season was running hot and heavy, but Candace had finally declared that enough was enough and shuttered the Leavenworth Hotshots for five days. Thirty days without a break, they were all so punchy that safety was becoming an issue.

Tori had thought about hanging out in town like usual. But she didn't want the noise and the bars. She wanted the quiet that a smokejumper had introduced her to an age ago.

By the time she parked her battered Toyota pickup beside the shiny Jeep Wrangler, Tori at least knew her destination. As if she hadn't looked up the access road on a topo map the moment she'd gotten off the Checker Mill Fire.

She spent most of the hour's hike up his trail telling herself she was being an idiot. A kiss, one bowl of chili, and one fire killed right at the very edge of a vegetable patch. That's all there was between them.

But each day on the fires since, she'd been watching

Candace and Luke. And each time she thought about the second kiss, the one after the fire—the more she knew that she at least had to answer the question that she and Colin had written between them.

The climb to his cabin followed a fast-running stream and then stretched out over a long green meadow. The fire had been killed in the woods. The last lines of trees stood green as well except for some char on the bark. For once, the fire's story had gone exactly as she'd predicted it.

His kiss had been a place of peace that had felt so right, so perfect. Part of it was the land, most of it was the man. The last of it was that he was the sort of man who had chosen this gorgeous stretch of mountainside for himself.

But how would he react to her arrival? Was he just being so thankful to be rescued from the fire that he'd have invited Medusa to come visit?

It had taken her a week after the Checker Mill Fire to make the mental connection. Tori had pulled one of Colin Steele's thrillers off her own bookshelf to discover that the man pictured on the back had introduced himself to her as Colin James.

And that had almost kept her away.

She didn't want to arrive as some sycophant, fan-girl no matter how much she enjoyed his novels. Yet here she was anyway, despite telling herself to stay away.

Tori almost turned from his front porch and headed back down the trail, which was beyond stupid. She closed her eyes, trudged up the steps, and struck out at the door.

There.

Now she'd knocked and there was no backing away without looking even beyond stupider than she felt. Stupiderist? Even by Ginger standards, this was extreme.

And she kept standing there.

And standing there.

She knocked again, harder.

Still nothing.

Well, she hadn't driven and hiked and nerved herself up to quit so easily. *Perseverance,* she reminded herself and stalked off to the back side of the cabin.

10

Colin looked up the moment she came into view. It was like that utterly impossible moment that always occurred between hero and heroine that he could never resist writing. First sight of each other at the same instant.

Even without the fire gear, he'd know her anywhere. There was a confidence, a surety to her stride unlike any other woman he'd ever known, or written. She came around the corner of his cabin as if she'd always been there, always belonged.

He stayed where he was and waited while she crossed the back porch, shed her pack, and came up into the vegetable garden. She wore hiking boots, shorts atop some of the longest legs he'd ever seen, and a light t-shirt luridly aflame, but patterned like a checker board. Across her chest it announced the Checker Mill Fire and the dates. The second date was the last time he'd seen her; twenty days and three hours.

His gaze finally made it up to her eyes as she arrived in front him.

"Great t-shirt."

"I brought one for you. You worked it too."

"Is that why you're here?"

"No. Nor is it because I know who you are."

Colin froze. Here it comes. All of the fantasy and hopes had just become meaningless.

"I've read a lot of your books. I thought you should know. I almost stayed away because of that."

"You what?" He hadn't expected that. "Then why are you here?"

She reached out and brushed her fingertips along his cheek. Not hot like fire, but rather cool like his stream, a caress that calmed and anchored him in this moment.

"You feel it too, don't you?" Tori asked softly.

He could only nod.

She closed the final step that separated them. When she slid her arms around his neck and kissed him, it was a scene right out of fiction. He'd never imagined anyone feeling so right in his arms.

Colin knew that Tori Ellison never stopped once she found what she wanted. She'd keep right on fighting fire or whatever came next in her life just as he'd always be writing.

When they lay down together on the garden path, he knew that he needed her as much as the blank page needed words. And their story would have many, many pages.

ROAD TO THE FIRE'S HEART

Wildfire engine driver Jill Conway-Jones *loves driving the big engines. But her real goal? Get up close and personal with a fire, just like the Interagency Hotshots. She gets a little too close when a burning tree crashes onto her fire engine.*

Hotshot Jess Monroe *loves the fire's heat, but can't seem to find a woman who sparks his own. At least not until he arrives to rescue the driver of the shattered truck—just in time to watch her kick out the windshield.*

And that's only the first turn on the Road to the Fire's Heart.

INTRODUCTION

This story comes from two sources.

First, Jess is the assistant superintendent of my Leavenworth Hotshot team from my first two Hotshot stories: *Fire Light, Fire Bright* and *The Firelights of Christmas*. It seemed to me that he was getting lonely what with his supervisor and his fellow assistant both finding true love in those previous stories.

Second, my sister once introduced me to a good friend of hers who was partnered with a top urban firefighter (both female). This was decades ago when women were still fighting for the legal right to even join a fire department; she was so good that she'd made captain in an atypically progressive department. Though they've been together for all this time, they've only recently gotten married—now that it's legal.

I also met their three-year-old (at the time) daughter.

That's where I found Jill—by wondering what my sister's friends' daughter was up to. She was in her mid-twenties by the time her moms were allowed to be married.

Rather than asking my sister, I wrote this story to find out. (I finally did ask and it turns out she's doing great, by the way, even if she didn't follow in her mom's firefighting footsteps.)

1

Squinting her eyes didn't help.

"Driving through pea soup would be easier."

As usual, Trent made no comment. Instead, he leaned closer to the wheel and also squinted out at the wildfire's thick smoke. He was trying to turn strong-silent type into a lifestyle as if that was a good thing. He also didn't deal well with abstract things like metaphors. He was a reliable enough partner, just not the most flexible.

A decent enough person, just kind of clueless and… such a guy. Despite his being two years older than her, she'd taken to thinking of herself as his big sister, taking care of him when he was being particularly ridiculous or pitiable without his even realizing it. His fire skills were good, so she didn't have to fix that, he was simply a social train wreck and needed a bit of a buffer from the world at large.

Jill Conway-Jones looked back out the windshield of their heavy-duty Type 4 wildfire engine—the big truck was only a year old and still shone despite her and Trent driving to several fires already this season. She wished she knew more about paintings so that she could say one of those educated sounding phrases about how the raging, fiery hell was so awful that only Matisse could have done it justice. But even as she thought it, she knew it was wrong. Her best friend from childhood was the hotshot New York City artist. Jill was just a hotshot.

Actually, that's what she wanted to be. At the moment she was a wildland firefighter and engine driver lost deep in the Cascade wilderness of who-knew-where central Washington. A wildfire engine driver, but it wasn't even her turn to drive. Trent was at the wheel and all she could do was try to figure out where they were.

US Forest Service fire road FS-273E was invisible, if that's what they were still on. Smoke was pouring across the road in thick black billows. Showers of brilliant orange sparks lit ash swirls from within as they blew by in vast clouds like the Monarch butterflies she'd once seen rising from a field of milkweed—a cloud of orange and black so thick that they seemed to block the sun.

Not that the sun was still aloft. She double-checked her watch, sunset should still be purpling the sky, but being deep within the steep mountains to all sides and the heavy smoke filling the valley, it was full night here. Wherever here was.

The headlights punched only a few feet into the smoke before reflecting back like high beams in fog.

They'd left the Stehekin River Valley Road what seemed hours ago. They were supposed to be delivering their seven hundred and fifty gallons of water to a beleaguered crew high up on Tolo Mountain. The one-lane dirt track had meandered up into the hills. The road's edge was sometimes carved out by rushing streams and at other times the entire lane was blocked by fallen trees. More than once they'd had to stop, pull out their chainsaws, and chop up eighty feet of flaming tree so that they could tug it out of the way with the truck's winch.

There was no turning around. No spot in the road to do so even if the hotshot crew hadn't needed their water. The wildfire engine was the only ground vehicle with a chance of making it out to them. The front cab looked like one of those heavy-duty delivery trucks and had the big growling diesel engine to match. The rear had slab sides covered with doors for tools and supplies. On the main bed was three tons of water and twice the firehose that any city firetruck could carry. They could even drive slow along a fire's perimeter and pump at the same time, a wildfire engine specialty that no city engine could match.

Jill loved this machine for its raw brute strength, but still wanted to test herself against the fire with the Interagency Hotshot Crews—the IHCs were the elite wildfire fighters, along with the smokejumpers, and she wanted to be a part of that.

Trent was hugging the cliff to her right on the inside edge of the lane, which was all they could do. After the third time a branch had slapped her rearview mirror flat against the side of the engine, she gave up readjusting it. Opening the window invariably filled the cabin with smoke and there wasn't anyone crazy enough to be behind them anyway.

Jill looked up at the cliff and tried to see any dips or ridges. Maybe by the topography she'd be able to locate some similar shape on the map spread across her lap.

Then she saw it coming toward her. She barely had time to scream—

"Log!"

—before the tree tumbled down the hill and slammed into the side of the engine. It was three feet in diameter and at least thirty feet long. And it was alive with flame down its entire length.

The tree slammed into the engine and knocked it sideways as if it weighed nothing. The Type 4 engine weighed eight tons. Between fuel, the water, and crew, the engine was loaded with an extra five tons. Despite all of their mass and the grip of the rear dualies, they were swept sideways across the road like a dust bunny trying to escape a flaming broom.

They tumbled off the other side of the road. Even as they rolled down the steep slope, she could see Trent trying to steer. At the moment they were upside down, the engine roaring; he must also be trying the gas.

Jill nearly strangled when the throttle-hold of adrenaline fear clamped her throat closed at the same moment she had the urge to giggle. The image of the truck lying on its back and waving its little four-wheel drive in the air wouldn't go away even as the cab's roof crumpled dangerously low making them both duck.

The engine continued to roll, one side per panicked gasp until she was nearly hyperventilating. Once right side up, the spinning tires slammed them forward only for a second. The engine stalled hard then they continued once more onto their back with a resounding crash.

They finally came to a rest with the driver's side door down.

She dangled above Trent, suspended by her seatbelt.

"Nice driving there, Ace." It was either laugh or scream, and she struggled to avoid the latter.

Trent didn't answer. Nor did he offer one of his trademark grunts.

Ahead of them, out the shattered windshield, there was nothing but the pitch dark of night. There was light coming in through the back window—dark, orange light that flickered ominously. She twisted around to look. The massive burning log lay in the back of the engine, at least one end of it. It was still burning which only added to the bad. Looking up and out her door, another massive branch lay across the remains of her window; the mirror was nowhere to be seen.

Her headlamp was still on her helmet which by some miracle was still on her head. She clicked it on. Trent was still breathing, but out cold. And his arm was at an angle that didn't look good at all.

Twisting herself around, she kicked at what was left of the windshield a few times with her boots until it broke free. The air outside the truck was marginally cooler than inside, which she took as a good sign.

Careful to brace herself so that she didn't fall on Trent, who still wasn't moving, she released her seatbelt. She crawled out to assess the situation. They were at the bottom of a dry ravine that hadn't been on fire. Parts of it now were, though, due to the log that had brought them here and it was bound to get worse shortly.

She leaned back in to extract Trent. Unable to release his seatbelt, she pulled out a knife and cut the straps, but it didn't help much. She weighed about one-twenty-five, and he weighed more like two-twenty-five.

"Great. We're alone, a bajillion miles from no one knows where," she told Trent's still form. "All the training drills in the world don't make me Supergirl."

"You sure?" A man's voice spoke close behind her.

2

The woman would have fallen over backward if Jess hadn't grabbed her about the waist. She wasn't a bad imitation of Supergirl at all. A blond ponytail hung out below her helmet. She stood two or three inches shorter than his own five-eight—he was still taller than Tom Cruise no matter how much he was teased on the fire line. And she was clad in full fire gear—which was always a turn-on. Firefighting women weren't as rare as they used to be, but ones fighting forest wildfires were still a very rare commodity.

He let go of her as soon as he was sure she had her balance once again.

"No, if I was Supergirl, I'd be able to lift my partner out by myself."

Jess tried not to sigh at the way she said partner. It sounded possessive. Bad luck for him, good luck for the dude still in the truck. Which was now on fire and they'd better get a move on.

He nudged Supergirl out of the way and ducked in to look at the situation. Her partner wasn't pinned but he had a busted arm. No way to assess anything else in this position, not in the time allowed. When Jess tucked the guy's bad arm into his half-open jacket, it didn't even elicit a grunt. Out cold. Jess grabbed the guy's lapels and gave a hard yank. He was big, but he slithered free like a sack of potatoes.

The woman ducked back into the truck through the windshield and emerged moments later with her gloves, a pair of burnover shelters, and the first aid kit. Keeping her head after what must have been a terrifying experience. Full points for that.

Jess had been scouting the edge of the fire. His hotshot crew was up the slope of the ravine trying to cut a line ahead of the blaze and he'd come down just in time to see the engine they'd been waiting for take the hit and tumble down into the ravine.

They'd both dragged the injured driver well clear, then he eyed the truck. There were a lot of supplies on there that they really needed. The flames weren't near the gas tanks yet and it seemed like a reasonable risk.

"Let's do some salvage."

He didn't have to tell her twice. With little ceremony she dropped one shelter and the first aid kit on her prostrate partner's chest. She clipped the other shelter to her belt and followed him back to the truck.

"Grab your PG bag."

"My what?"

"Personal gear."

The fire was bright enough to see the blank look on her face. *Right.* She probably drove a city engine most of time; she wouldn't know hotshot lingo.

"Food, water, stuff like that."

"Oh," she ducked in and came back out with a small knapsack and a Pulaski fire axe. Okay, not all city. Only wildland firefighters used the tool that was an axe on one side and an adze on the other.

In moments they'd grabbed a five-gallon cube of water and two more of gas for the chainsaws. He snagged a twenty-pound bag of foodstuffs and wished he had time to riffle through more of the doomed engine's lockers. It was trashed anyway, not even worth trying to use its own pump and water supply to put itself out. He'd expected to find two bodies as he approached the cab. And then Supergirl had kicked out the windshield.

She came back out with a stretcher for her partner.

"Let's get clear." In three ferry loads, they put another couple hundred feet between them and the now engulfed engine. They stood in the ashen forest with their salvaged gear and her partner on a stretcher. Jess waited, but even now that they were relatively safe, she didn't slide into shock.

"How bad is the road up to here?"

She looked at him like he was an idiot, which wouldn't surprise anyone, him least of all.

"I mean for an ambulance."

"We don't—" then she looked grim for a moment and glanced down at her partner where he lay strapped into the stretcher. "I don't even know where we are. Visibility was near zero for the last hour."

Jess clicked on the radio, "Candace? Jess here."

"Wondering when you'd get off your lazy ass and check in."

Supergirl had a cute giggle.

"Aww, you missed me. I'm touched. I've got a rollover wildfire engine here at the bottom of the ravine in sector two-six. It's—" there was a loud boom that had both him and Supergirl ducking. She lay over her partner to protect him which was just too sweet for words. "It's toast. That column of flame about a mile to your southeast was one of the gas tanks breaching. Need a medevac and the road is impassible. Got any helos on call?"

"Hold. I'll check."

He turned to Supergirl as she sat back up and began brushing wood chips and other detritus that was falling back down from the explosion off her partner. The engine was a complete loss, but she spared it little more than a glance. He'd seen it before, women so focused on their families that they barely thought about their own safety during evacuations.

"You have a name?"

"Jill Conway-Jones a.k.a. Supergirl."

Sense of humor despite whatever shock she was in. Stretcher boy was one lucky guy; Jess wondered which one of them was Conway and which was Jones. He could see her more clearly now by the light of the burning engine. Seriously lucky guy.

"I'm Jess Monroe. I'm an assistant super on the Leavenworth Interagency Hotshot Crew that's currently up that ridge cutting line. We'll get you and your boyfriend out of here in a minute."

"He's—"

"Jess?" The radio crackled to life sparing him whatever happy domestic story she was going to spill all over him. "Candace here. You're getting lucky tonight, boyo. I've got a Jeannie Clark in Firehawk Oh-Three from MHA heading your way. Give her a beacon. ETA in one minute, she's just finished a dump run and is turning your way. Then get back up here. Please tell me you salvaged some saw fuel."

"Water and food too."

"Love you, Monroe. Swear to god I do."

"You can show me some of that lovin' when I get there.

Out." And he began fishing out the infrared beacon. It would show up far brighter in the helicopter pilot's night-vision goggles than a normal flashlight. He hoped that Luke had his radio tuned in for that transmission; Candace's husband was so much fun to poke at. He'd been a hotshot for a year now and married to their super for six months, but it still took him a beat or two to keep up with her. It took all of them that, because Candace rocked the job of leading the team.

The next ten minutes were busy. The helo coming in overhead drowned any conversation beneath the heavy pounding of the big rotors. A guy came down through thick branches on a penetrator winch and helped them hook up the stretcher.

Winch guy took a moment to unsling a camera and snap shots of the burning engine and of Jess and Supergirl double-checking on Trent.

"Be back down for you in a minute," the helo guy shouted to Jill.

"No," she yelled back. "I'm uninjured. I'm sure they can use another firefighter here."

Jess was about to protest.

"I've got my Firefighter I and II, I've been driving wildfire engines for three seasons, and I've got my red card for wildfire." She pointed at the three cubes of fuel and water, "And do you want to carry all those up the hill yourself?"

At forty pounds per cube, he wasn't looking forward to it.

3

"ast chance," the helicopter guy shouted.

Jill waved him aloft, not giving the hotshot a chance to insist. No way was she passing up a chance to work with an IHC crew. Especially not for the sake of Trent who would probably be an engine driver forever. He was headed for what he needed, med care; now it was time to head for what she needed, fire.

In minutes, Trent and the photographer were back aboard the helicopter and the pounding of the rotor blades was fading away.

Funny that the hotshot thought she and Trent were an item.

Jess Monroe was awfully cute. And she'd felt his easy strength when she stumbled and ended up in his arms. Her knees had been shaky from the crash, but after he'd held her, even for that brief moment, she'd felt so much more stable. Too bad he was already taken by his supervisor.

Giving a man too much time to think was never a good idea. So she slipped her Pulaski through the loops on her knapsack…no, her PG bag, and slung it over her shoulders. Then she looped the salvaged food bag over her head.

With a shrug, Jess picked up one of the fuel cubes and the water cube, leaving her the other fuel cube. That was decent of him; five gallons of fuel weighed nine pounds less than the forty-three of the water cubes.

"Ready?" His voice didn't sound at all tight from the heavy load he was now holding.

She scanned the ground, took one last look at the burning engine, trying not to think about the paperwork involved in that loss, and nodded for him to lead the way. She'd miss the engine; it had been a fun machine to drive—had actually made her feel a little like she *was* Supergirl, womanhandling thirteen tons of firefighting beast.

The first hundred feet across the ravine floor went quickly enough. The next hundred, starting up the steep hillside toward the hotshot crew, felt okay too. Then she put her head down and tackled the job of putting one foot in front of the other. In minutes she was drenched in sweat and her arms had started complaining about the load.

Jess led slow and steady, but without stopping and she didn't want to complain, especially as he was carrying thirty more pounds than she was. As they climbed farther into the trees, the orange light from behind faded. A stolen glance showed that they'd climbed a thousand feet or more up from the ravine. The mountains beyond glowed in a hundred shades of red and orange. To the north, flames leapt gold-orange toward the sky. To the south, it was a lower, more sullen burn in deep reds. All else was dark, the forest with night and the sky with thick clouds of smoke. If the helicopter returned, she didn't spot it.

Turning back to the trees, she saw that Jess was well ahead of her now and she did what she could to catch up with him. He had a strong, steady persistence to him.

She wished she had the breath to ask him questions, but she'd left the ability to speak far down the slope.

Instead, she focused her headlamp on the ground in front of her. A simple rhyme formed in her head as she climbed. It so exactly matched the pace of her steps that she was unable to eradicate it.

Jess and Jill went up the hill,
With damned heavy pails of water…

*J*ess had tried to burn her out on the hike up. He wasn't completely sure of his own motivations. It wasn't as if there would be any easy way to evacuate her if she reached the fire line and then wanted to go home. The only crews who worked farther from base on a fire than the hotshots were the smokejumpers. The smokies went where there were no roads at all. The hotshots drove to the end of the road and then hiked in with nothing but the saws and axes on their backs. The fact that now they were only a half mile from a forest road was the closest they'd been to civilization in five days, having started well to the west.

But every time he glanced back to check on her, Jill Conway-Jones was still there behind him. Sometimes closer, sometimes farther back, and once stopped and turned to stare out at the forest. She hadn't even set down her heavy load, just stood staring out at the wonder of it all.

It was one of the best parts of being a hotshot and it

surprised him—and made him like her even more—that she appreciated the land.

The work was brutal, the hours and pay sucked, but to stand out in vast stretches of wilderness and observe the ever-changing landscape was worth almost any price. He hadn't expected some engine driver to understand.

He'd finally turned away from watching Jill watch the fire and continued up the slope. He was always building stupid fantasies in his head and she was just another opportunity make up false dreams.

Jess had never held a fantasy about Candace, or Patsy the team's other assistant super, even before they each had married. But it was still his trademark. Build a ton of stupid dreams and then watch them shatter as reality got in the way. Beautiful blond Supergirl firefighter falls into his arms, sure, but really is partner with someone named Trent. He guessed it was close enough to Clark Kent, but that didn't mean he had to like it. The compound last name put the final stamp on his stupidity.

His legs and arms were burning as he crested another rise and stepped into an unexpected clearing of grass and slash. Three steps later before he could stop himself, he stumbled on a passed-out hotshot and landed full upon him.

"Uh," Luke grunted. "Can't I even get a nap without you crawling in with me? Been waiting on you, Jess. You got any fuel on you?"

Jess rolled off him, too exhausted to speak. The last thousand feet his arms had burned like demons and his attention had tunneled until each step became his whole world. Instead, he thudded his knuckles against one of the cubes.

"Good job, bro," Candace's husband rolled to his feet,

something Jess was incapable of at the moment. "Just remember to keep your mind off my woman," Luke paid him back for the earlier tease over the radio with a friendly slap on the shoulder that almost tumbled him back to the lying on the ground. Then Luke headed off in the other direction carrying the fuel cube as if it didn't weigh a thing. He didn't take the water cube. Yet more payback—still worth it.

Now if he could just lie here for a minute until his arms stopped screami—

Jill!

He'd forgotten about her for the last part of the climb. How far behind had he left her? That was rude as hell no matter what he'd been thinking.

He jerked to his feet, spun—and ploughed head on into Jill. Once again he landed on top of a firefighter in the grass.

Jess tried to roll off her but was blocked by the fuel cube she'd been carrying that now lay beside her. He started to roll the other way, but she stopped him.

"You roll onto the food bag after I carried it all this way, you're going to end up being a very dead firefighter."

"Right, sorry." Though it was hard to be completely sorry, lying on top of her, with their faces inches apart and lit by the side glow from their headlamps. He'd been right before how pretty she was. It wasn't just the blond ponytail. She had bright blue eyes and an open face—presently covered with smears of smoke.

"Are you going to be getting up soon or are you just planning to lie there trying to pretend there isn't a fire coming?"

"Uh," he climbed off her and gave her a hand up. "I was just coming back down to—" But she was already here.

"To rescue the poor waif?" She ignored his offer to

give her a hand up. "What part of 'I'm a firefighter' didn't you get?"

"The part where you're tougher than I am."

"I'm not tough," she dusted off her Nomex fire-resistant pants and shirt as if he'd somehow dirtied them. Then she fired an absolutely radiant smile at him that almost knocked him to the ground again, "I'm just stubborn as all get out."

5

And if she wasn't, Jill would have had the good sense to have grabbed that helicopter ride and flown out with Trent. It had taken everything she had and more to conquer that ravine's slope with fifty pounds of fuel and food in addition to her own gear. But she'd done it and now that she was here, there wasn't a chance that they were going to find her wanting.

"So," she looked at Jess. He still inspected her wide-eyed as if she'd transported down off an alien ship rather than just battled up a mountain in his silent wake. "Are we good to go?" She didn't even know if she could lift a kitten at this point, never mind a Pulaski.

"Sure," he picked up both his remaining water cube—she'd seen the bobbing light of someone carrying Jess' fuel toward the fire line—and her fuel cube. She was about to call after him that she could carry her own damned fuel, but wasn't sure if she could so she kept her mouth shut. Shouldering the food sack, she followed in his wake.

The night was quiet here.

A chainsaw coughed to life close ahead and then another. In moments they were biting wood.

Okay, it was a relatively quiet night. At least there was no roaring truck engine or even louder fire. The night here was truly dark outside of their helmet lights. The smoke clouds far above glowed the deep red of reflected fire light, but it wasn't bright enough to cast any light over the scene.

What she'd initially taken for a clearing was one end of a fire break. It stretched for a half a mile along the ridgetop. The line had been cut, the branches dragged away, and, once they reached the far side of the cleared line, they were walking on a stretch a dozen yards wide that had been scraped down to deep soil or rock. There were no machines up here, not this high up the mountain. Unbelievably, this had all been done by hand.

Maybe she wasn't ready to be a hotshot.

They reached the far end of the cleared line. Here the chainsaws were hard at work. A line of soot-covered workers followed close behind them dragging away branches.

Jess stopped by a woman wrestling an impossibly large branch into submission.

"Jess! Thanks for the fuel. Helo's down for the night and they didn't bring any gas in the last supply run."

Jill recognized the voice from the earlier radio exchange. The voice had given no impression of the woman. In person, Candace the team's superintendent looked all-powerful. Smeared with dirt and smoke char, sawdust caught in her hair, she looked like Superwoman making Jill's own Supergirl feel more like Supertoddler.

"I've got a tag-a-long," Jess set down the cubes he was carrying but didn't even have the decency to hug his girlfriend.

Jill moved up beside him and shoved him hard on the

shoulder. Unable to step high enough to clear the cube he'd set down, he fell sideways into the cleared dirt.

"I am not a tag-a-long," she practically shouted down at him. "I'm a firefighter." She looked back up at Candace who was watching her with a half smile. "I'm no hotshot, but I've got my red card," Jill said it more quietly this time.

"Well, let's see what kind of a hotshot you make." Candace didn't hold out a hand, leaving Jess to struggle back to his feet as she spoke to him. "She's attached to your hip. Teach her. Safety, procedures, whole thing by the manual. Start with swamping."

"Okay," Jess didn't sound very happy about it, but it was more than Jill had even hoped for—a tryout on a live fire. He headed toward the sound of chainsaws punctuated by the sharp crack of a falling tree.

Candace stopped her before Jill could follow along and looked at her with an intensity that was alarming for a moment, then she smiled brilliantly, her teeth bright in comparison to her char-stained face.

"That one needs a lesson or two in humility. Kick his ass, sister."

Before Jill could respond, Candace had once again clamped onto her branch and was dragging it off into the trees.

For the next twelve hours, she and Jess did just that.

"Swamping. It's called swamping the branches, not dragging."

"Why?"

Jess paused and laughed, making her stumble on the branch he'd been dragging just in front of her. "I haven't a clue. But it's swamping. That much you can trust me on."

As they worked back and forth across the fire line, following behind the sawyers, they spared a some breath to talk. Jess told her about his degree in Psychology.

"Never was much at research and I sure didn't want to spend my life listening to other people's problems. I don't know what I was thinking. It was interesting and I met some good friends, but being indoors wasn't my idea of living. I met Candace in a coffee shop. She was from a firefighting family and she made it sound so amazing. She and I worked crews all over the west. When she got the call to form up a new team and tapped me for assistant super, it was just about the best day of my life. It was like I really knew I'd done something."

The way he talked about Candace was a curious mixture of humbling and daunting. The more he talked about her, the more imposing the super became. He clearly worshipped the ground she walked on. But it was also a little bit odd. He only spoke of her in relation to firefighting. How she'd done recruitment in a way he'd never seen before. How she kept everyone's spirits up even after a two-day cut on a fire line that was overrun. He never once said anything about their relationship.

"I came from a firefighting family," she told him, but Jill never had much to say beyond that. She came from a line of firewomen. She was the only daughter of two of Seattle's first female fire officers. That she was straight didn't bother her moms; they had made her various boyfriends welcome over the years. And her birth mom's father, Grampa Jones, had been one as well. Jill had served with her parents awhile, but felt overshadowed by them. They were both such strong, outgoing personalities that Jill had feared she was becoming invisible in her own quiet way.

They'd been surprised when she'd signed up for the wildland engine crew. But if they'd been hurt, they didn't show it. Instead, for her birthday they'd given her tuition for both emergency vehicle training and the expensive

CDL—the commercial driver's license wasn't required but they had gotten it for her anyway. Neither of which would have saved her from the rolling tree that had wiped out their engine even if she'd been at the wheel.

She kept quiet on the details of her firefighting family because she'd learned over the years that most guys didn't understand about growing up with two mothers, so she kept that fact to herself.

She hadn't gone to college. She'd been a Junior Fireman in high school and gone straight into the academy for three months to earn her firefighter certifications. There had never been any question about what she'd do, only what her particular path to fire would be. Listening to Jess Monroe talk about Candace Cantrell was definitely giving her ideas.

6

———

*J*ess couldn't get a feel for Jill Conway-Jones. He remembered down at the wrecked engine that she'd been funny. But up here on the line, she was mostly quiet. When she spoke, it was to ask him about hotshotting.

They switched over to grubbing a twenty-foot line, which was just as exciting as it sounded. It was working the dirt with a Pulaski until there was nothing living in a swath that was hopefully wide enough to stop a fire from crossing—not even organic duff was allowed to remain. The cut trees would force the fire down to the ground, the removal of the branches and underbrush would rob it of fuels to slow it further, and the grubbed line would hopefully stop it cold.

But for everything she didn't say, she more than made up for by doing. She'd tirelessly leaned into branches that must have weighed more than she did. And, once she got the proper Pulaski technique, she kept up with him right down the line.

The more he did manage to get from her, the more he

cursed the luck of Trent the engine driver, whether he was Conway or Jones. A woman like her didn't come along even every year, never mind every day.

He did finally poke around enough to rediscover her funny side.

"Supergirl is trying to be superhotshot," Jess had forgotten his early nickname for her until they'd worked through the whole night and a dirty, smoking dawn was approaching.

"No, she's actually trying not to be superlame."

"She'd can't be," Jess insisted in between slices with the Pulaski—he had to chop out a stubborn root. "That job description has already been taken by me. Only one allowed per team."

"Fine. You want the title, it's yours," the smile he could hear in her voice through the exhaustion just made him like her all the more. "I'll get myself a t-shirt to prove it. It'll have the red and yellow S on it and then in tiny letters, I'll have it say, '…and, yes, he is with me'."

Almost too exhausted to breathe, she still gave him the energy to laugh.

When sunrise finally did happen, they'd sat on a cut log to rest through a breakfast break of energy bars, an orange, and a canteen of water with electrolyte powder.

"Yum! You hotshots really know how to live the high life."

Jess grimaced, "Just wait until the fire gets here. This has all been prep."

As if in answer to her question, the first air tanker of the morning raced by low overhead, dumping a long line of red retardant on the line of trees beyond the firebreak. Wouldn't do to have some errant spark, of which there would be plenty to hunt down and kill during the height of the battle, ignite the fire beyond the fire line.

7

"How's our tag-a-long doing?" Candace walked up to where she and Jess were still eating on the log. Beside her was one of the sawyers, a big handsome guy she hadn't met yet. Candace put enough sarcasm in her voice that Jill knew she was being teased.

Jess groaned as if wounded to the core and Jill had to fight to suppress a laugh. His constant energy and sense of fun was all that had kept her upright through a brutal night's work.

"I think *I'm* now the tag-a-long," Jess whined like an old man. "Jill doesn't know the meaning of slow down. Picks up technique faster than any recruit who's ever crossed our lines."

"He's been a great teacher," Jill put in. His constant fine-tuning, even long after exhaustion had them both staggering, had revealed a drive for excellence that matched her own and a style of patient teaching that she could only hope to learn some day.

"She learns even faster than you, big guy," he addressed the sawyer.

"No way!" The guy faced her squarely. "Okay, lady. That means it's you and me for the fire. Then we'll see how you do."

Jill couldn't tell if he was teasing or serious. He was an imposing man. Like one of those military clichés with the manly jaw and the broad shoulders.

"Aren't men just the cutest things?" Then Candace pulled him into a kiss.

And not just some friendly peck either.

Jill startled and looked from them to Jess to see how he was taking it. Rather than angry, he looked…jealous?

"Come on you two. Do you have to keep proving how happy you are? Get a room, go behind a tree, something."

The big guy broke off and looked down at Candace, "We've got to get him a lady."

Jill was still trying to catch up with what was happening. Jess wasn't with Candace? The big guy was?

That explained why he'd only talked about Candace on the fires, because that's what she and Jess did together— team superintendent and assistant.

Jill had to sift through all the stories he'd told about their meeting and working together. If they weren't a couple, everything shifted to show his huge respect for a strong woman. She'd thought he was putting his lover up on some silly pedestal, ready to fall.

"How about you, lady?" The big guy looked down at her. "You in the market for a slightly used hotshot? He's kinda scruffy, but we all like him well enough."

"No, she's got a guy, the broken arm we medevaced out last night. Her name's Jill," Jess offered. "Jill, this char-monkey is Luke. But we call him Mud to keep his ego in check." Then he leaned close as if to whisper in confidence, "Doesn't help."

Jill felt cornered until she caught Candace's sly smile.

Here were two men who thought that a strong woman was an asset—not just an asset, but absolutely worth seeking out and following. Jill had been raised by two of the strongest women that she'd ever met, ones she'd spent her whole life trying to make proud.

And she'd bet that both of her moms would love these three.

Here they were, three magnificent firefighters, standing as friends for a moment in the dawn light before turning to face the approaching flames.

Could there be any place that she'd rather be?

Then she turned to look at Jess. Considerate, passionate…single. He'd spent the whole night telling her about his life and how much he loved what he did and the people he did it with. She'd learned less about some boyfriends in six months than she'd learned about him in the last dozen hours. Jess had blown poor Trent out of the water in the first thirty seconds when he'd caught her and laughed at one of her jokes.

Jill looked at Candace, "Need another hotshot?" What would have been a ridiculous question a dozen hours ago felt completely normal now.

Candace simply held out a hand and they shook on it. Deal. Done.

Yes!

She could really get to enjoy working for a woman like her.

She looked back up at Luke.

"Scruffy hotshot slightly used? Might work for me," she poked Jess in the arm as if she was testing a side of beef. "How about this one? Think he's interested?"

She'd never been so forward in her life, but the way his muscles felt, she'd have to do it more often.

Jess was blinking at her, trying just as hard to catch up.

"Trent was my *fire* partner, Jess," she offered the missing clue.

He kept blinking at her in surprise.

"Not the quickest one is he?" Jill glanced up at Candace.

"He's fast enough under normal conditions. But like all the really good ones," Candace went up on her toes to kiss Luke on his cheek, "you can knock them into stunned puppy land pretty easily."

Jill decided to help Jess along, since she was the one being forward.

He had called her Supergirl after all.

She leaned over and kissed him.

It took Jess Monroe about two more seconds and then he caught on very well indeed. In moments the exhaustion that had been coursing through her body like an aching pulse beat was replaced with a sizzling heat.

"Maybe," Luke drawled out, "we should get one of the helos to do a water drop on these two; cool the fire down a bit."

Maybe, Jill thought to herself, but she didn't think it would make any difference at all.

A HOTSHOT CHRISTMAS

***Heavy equipment driver Sheila Williams** got blown up one too many times. The Army kicked her loose for that idiot reason. How the hell she ended up in a tourist town for the holidays makes even less sense.*

***Hotshot Randall Jones** fights wildfires for a living. The adrenaline fits him like a fire in the forest.*

They both feel the heat in A Hotshot Christmas.

INTRODUCTION

I wanted to end the series with a bang. This was to be my last Hotshot short story, my last Firehawks short story, and actually, my last Firehawks tale of any kind—the last Firehawks novel, *Wild Fire,* was written earlier and released only a dozen days after this story. Of course it turned out that fire wasn't done with me, even if I thought I was done with it. But the Oregon Firebirds were still an undreamed-of series waiting two years in the future.

I had such fun writing a previous Hotshot Christmas story, *The Firelights of Christmas,* that I definitely wanted to try another. Leavenworth, Washington (where my fictional team is based) is a delightful tourist village—pleasant enough that I've considered moving there a couple of times. And the most fun time of year there is Christmas. Yes, it's tourist madness. But it is also vibrantly alive and filled with bright sun, deep snow, and a close camaraderie among the locals who actually reside there.

I wanted to celebrate that. I wanted to roll around in it and have fun.

My answer?

I dropped a character into the midst of the scene who hates the town and the crowds and Christmas and…

She's not Ms. Scrooge. She's a soldier who can't understand the strange world she encounters once she's out of the Army.

Sheila was born from a conversation I had years ago with a soft-spoken female Black Hawk crew chief who had left the Army after serving four years and two tours in Iraq.

"It's so strange. No one pays my rent. No one makes my food. I never had to pay bills because I enlisted straight out of high school. I try to explain my confusion of having to make so many choices, but it doesn't make sense to any civilians. You're so used to it. My buddies are all still inside and they don't understand either. It's so hard you can't begin to imagine."

Sheila is my attempt to understand, and to give that crew chief a happy ending that I've since heard she found.

One further note on this story. As I write, I often laugh and sometimes cry as I write. But every now and then I write a story that just gives me chills (in a good way). And sometimes I read a story after it's done and I wonder how I managed to write that. This is one of those stories; a great way to finish a series.

1

Sheila inspected the heavy dark beams and white plaster of the restaurant. A hostess—in a bad Bavarian costume of ruffled sleeves, low-cut above blousy, cotton-cupped breasts—smiled at her as she sashayed across the hardwood floor in incongruous heels.

"Table for one?" Just one notch too perky for her to swallow.

"No, thanks. Just looking in." Sheila turned abruptly and nearly trampled a couple and their kids coming in the door. *Civilians! Too close!* She kept the epithet to herself and stepped around them and back out into the crisp darkness.

To her left was the snow sprinkled faux-Bavarian town of Leavenworth, Washington, so perfect it was like a goddamn life-sized snow globe. To her right was a McDonald's with a wood and plaster Germanic facade. She'd promised herself that she'd do better than McD's for a Thanksgiving Day dinner, but crowds were kind of a problem for her and the town was packed.

Saddle up, girl.

She didn't even bother raising her camo jacket's collar

as she turned to tromp through the snow—even the damned falling snow was picturesque—and into the heart of the town. Somewhere there had to be a bar with a burger, a brew, and a minimum of Bavarian.

She'd been driving to…well, nowhere. She'd been driving *away* from the family Thanksgiving in Seattle. Five hours through packed city roads and over slick mountain ones.

Not a soul understood what it meant that she was out of the Army. No one got that a TBI diagnosis didn't mean she was nuts. Traumatic Brain Injury meant that she'd been blown up one too many times for the Army to trust her at the wheel of her big transport truck. Didn't meant she was crazy. Please let it not mean she was crazy.

Which totally explained why she was in a resort town, that looked about as inauthentic as most of the ones in the real Bavaria did, looking for a quiet place to get drunk on Thanksgiving night.

A polka band playing out on the town's square made her wonder how the tuba player's lips didn't freeze to his mouthpiece. Children skidded around despite all the salt and sand laid down on the sidewalks. One ran into her legs hard enough to fall back on its butt.

She stopped, knelt down, and picked up the kid to put it back on its feet. *See, acting perfectly normal. Helping out.*

It took one look at her, burst out crying, and raced away.

Sheila closed her eyes for a moment…before standing and continuing through town. She crossed the street to get clear of the square.

Bavarian Bistro. Not a chance.

Soup Cellar. *O Tannenbaum* playing on the juke because Thanksgiving was over in another half dozen hours. She didn't even make it halfway down the stairs.

She closed her eyes to get past the garish Christmas store and let the tourists bounce off her until she was clear.

King Ludwig's. The Mad King. Not a freaking chance.

She jostled and was nudged along until she fell out the other end of the town. Four blocks. She'd survived four blocks. *Sometimes the victories are small.* She hated when the psychs were right, especially when it felt more like defeat.

At the far end of the tourist strip, the town collapsed back into small American town. Dimly lit, cold. She leaned against the concrete wall of a closed warehouse and did what she could to catch her breath.

"Been following you," a deep male voice.

She really didn't need this shit right now. She rested her hand on her sidearm, but the Glock 19 wasn't on her hip where it should be. Where it *used* to be.

"No need for that," the voice continued as she started a hand up to her concealed shoulder carry. Her back was turned, he shouldn't have been able to spot her motion.

Sheila risked a glance.

Big guy. Ten feet back. Standing planted on the sidewalk. No one behind or to the sides. Alone. She recognized the stance.

"You got somewhere to be?" His voice was soft, steady. She could deal with that. "I can help you get there."

Sheila could only shake her head. No, she had nowhere to be. Might never again.

He waited a while before continuing, like he was studying her and thinking.

"What?"

"Got a place you might like."

"Shit! Not looking for a goddamn roll in the hay."

"More like snow, this time of year," he said it with barely a hint of smile. "Besides, it's not that kinda place. And my wife would kick my ass."

"Must be some tough wife to keep you on a short leash."

He shrugged, "Works for me."

Sheila stared at him, but he just waited. Military recognized military. She could do worse. She offered him a shrug. Didn't really matter anyway.

He pointed past her.

She waved for him to lead the way.

Being a smart man, he also saw that he should circle wide out onto the empty street rather than try to come by her on the sidewalk.

2

Randall sat close beside Jess and Jill. They were about the funniest damn couple on the whole team and who better to sit with while Thanksgiving dinner was cooking. The two Js met on a wildfire in the middle of last season and Jess had somehow swept her up before she'd even hit the damned fire line. Or maybe she'd swept him up. Randall had long since learned that being five-four, blond, and cute as hell had nothing to do with Jill's skills. The woman totally rocked it, offering her sunny smile the whole time.

"Sure you don't have a twin sister?" He asked for the hundredth time.

"Nope! My moms only had the one kid."

"Crap!" They shared a smile. He'd met her moms at the wedding, two of Seattle's finest firefighters.

A cold gust of air crawled up his back.

"Close the goddamn door!" Randall shivered. He really should move, but this crew area of the Leavenworth fire station was maxed out. The volunteer firefighters and their families would have made it crowded enough. But Captain Cantrell had invited his daughter's entire Interagency Hotshot Crew to his Thanksgiving Feed. No wildfires in the winter in the Cascade Mountains, but half of them had found ways to keep busy and keep local. Candace was the kind of superintendent who helped make good things like that happen.

"Happy Thanksgiving to you too, asshole," Luke smacked him on top of the head as he came through the door and they both laughed.

Then a shadow slipped in behind him and did close the door. She was close to six feet, not gaunt, but not far from it. She had dark hair that fell in soft waves past her shoulders and narrowed her pale face even more. Her fists were jammed deep in the pockets of her unzipped hunting jacket. She wore a turtleneck and a thin white sweater that flowed down her slender frame, apparently oblivious to the biting cold.

She wasn't exactly beautiful, but she was as dramatic as hell.

"What's your problem?" Her voice was low, rough.

"Breathing around you," was all Randall managed.

Somewhere in the background Jill laughed. He couldn't tell whether or not it was at him, but he sure wasn't going to risk looking away to find out. She might evaporate if he did, or stab him.

Her dark eyes studied him for a long moment, then glanced aside to look out the door's frosted window.

"Sorry. Rude. I know. Never think first. You'll have to get used to that if you're going to hang around me. I'm Randall. Randall Jones," he held out a hand.

Again those piercing eyes studied him for a long moment. Then she cursed emphatically.

He started to draw back his hand, but she reached out and shook it once. Solidly. With a damned strong grip. And her fingers were cold as ice.

"Sorry. I'm having trouble around people at the moment."

"Oh, then you're fine here. No people at all. Only firefighters and a couple folks stupid enough to marry them." *And you're babbling, dude. Rein it in.*

"Okay," and the ghost actually smiled—a thin one, but definitely there. It looked amazing on her. "As long as there aren't any actual people."

"Scout's honor," he did his best Boy Scout three-fingered salute.

She snapped upright and was most of the way to a hard salute before she froze, went momentarily wide-eyed, then rammed her fist back into her pocket hard enough that he was surprised she didn't punch through the fabric.

"Sorry," he didn't know what else to say. "I'm…" Maybe it would be better if he just introduced her around or… "Are you hungry? We can go see if it's done cooking." Even though he could see by the long table that the turkeys weren't out yet.

She studied him again, then glanced sideways at Luke.

Randall hadn't even noticed that he was still there, watching them.

Luke gave a shrug to her as if to say, "Up to you."

Sheila turned back to him. Again that long pause before she spoke, as if she had to practice it in her head first before speaking.

"Food would be okay," she finally managed. "A beer sure wouldn't hurt."

Searching for a possible path through the crowd, and seeing the way his ghost was still hanging close to the door, he decided for expediency. He grabbed his jacket off the back of his chair.

"It's quieter that way," he pointed out the door.

Again, her first look went to Luke, who nodded that it would be okay.

He held the door for her and led her outside.

3

Randall's grip had been strong, solid. What Sheila would expect from a firefighter.

"Were you a SEAL too? Like Luke." He asked as he led her toward the back of the building. It was dark except for the distant lights of the town reflecting off the snow, but the path was shoveled. She could smell the thick pine of the trees growing close behind the station.

He didn't move like a trained hand-to-hand fighter. She'd wager she could take him down if necessary, even without her sidearm.

Shoulder carry, not hip. She still needed to change that habit.

"He's a SEAL?" That fit. The silence and the arrogant level of self-assuredness. An unarmed man who simply said, "No need for that," as she'd prepared to draw on him. SEAL? Unarmed? Not likely. "No. Not like Luke. There aren't any SEAL women. I was in the Army. A HEMTT driver."

"A what?"

"Big trucks. A Heavy Expanded Mobility Tactical

147

Truck. Also just called a 'heavy.' I carried anything lighter than an Abrams tank." That shut up most men.

"Did you like it?"

Not Randall. He continued on cheerfully as if they were having an actual conversation and it was okay that she'd driven a massive Army transport for a living…until she couldn't anymore.

He held open a door for her at the rear of the building and she saw that they were entering the back of an equipment bay. A line of shining fire trucks and a pair of polished ambulances were lined up in a neat row. At the far end, one of the doors was rolled halfway up and she could see some guys standing around a big closed-top grill nosed just outside the open door. No crowd pressure in the vast bay which was a good thing. By their feet was a cooler and most of them were nursing a beer. *Target acquired.*

"Yeah," she looked at the beautiful rigs all lined up. "I liked it a lot." Maybe too pretty for her taste. She preferred a machine built to get down and dirty, but the ladder truck could definitely tempt her.

He led her up to the group.

"Captain Cantrell," he began introducing her around. "And Candace is the super on our IHC team."

Father-daughter. Obvious right down to how they stood—sure of themselves but without any real ego display.

"You met her husband Luke."

Which explained just who could keep a SEAL on that short leash.

"And this is Patsy, one of our two foremen. Her husband's the town baker and is around somewhere."

Again, a solid grip and a questioning eye. IHC. Interagency Hotshot Crew. That meant that Randall wasn't just some firefighter. He walked into the wilderness to fight wildfires with a chainsaw and an axe—a very real form of hand-to-hand combat. She suspected it took some serious balls despite his easygoing manner. It also meant "team," which explained the outsider looks she was getting. They were being nice about it though, so she tamped down any need to get out. Especially when "out" would mean going back among the flocks of happy tourists. Families. Candace handed her a beer from the cooler so she'd definitely stick for a bit.

"And I still don't know your name. Sorry." Firefighter Randall Jones was a guy who couldn't stop apologizing. Very strange.

"Sheila Williams."

"And this is Sheila," he introduced her to everyone else.

He didn't mention the Army, which she appreciated. But he did mouth her name a few times to himself to make sure he had it down. Which was kind of cute.

4

Randall shadowed her the whole evening. At first because he wanted to, but later she seemed to appreciate it. She didn't exactly open up, but she did appear to relax. When a plate was offered piled high with grilled turkey and all the fixings, she took it. When he pointed to the fire station donation box and told her they were all kicking in a ten, she slipped in a twenty.

Luke floated by on occasion, but made no big deal of it. He'd expected to lose her to Luke, some form of ex-military bonding, but Sheila didn't seem inclined to leave his side which worked fine for him. Even if it was just for the evening, it was nice to have a date. Of sorts. Eventually she told him the story of the Seattle family dinner she'd bugged out of. He couldn't get her to laugh, but he raised that soft smile a couple of times and called it good.

Sheila hung around right through the cleanup chores, earning her a round of thanks that she did her best to shrug off.

"Where are you staying? I'll walk you there."

She shrugged, "Gotta find a room. And I know how to walk myself just fine."

"Won't find one on a Thanksgiving in Leavenworth." Randall glanced at Luke who seemed to be making a point of not watching them. "I've got a couch. Not much of a place, but you're welcome to it."

She didn't do that sideways check-in with Luke that had punctuated so much of the evening. Instead she looked at him carefully. "Just the couch."

His nod of agreement settled it, at least until they were headed to his place through the cold night air. It was late enough that all of the tourists had gone to bed. He liked the town at these times—still all bedazzled up, but only the occasional local walking by with a friendly nod and a "Hey."

"No luggage?"

She swung open her still unzipped coat, fists again in pockets. "Left in a bit of a hurry." By the sound of her family dinner, he would have too.

"I can lend you a t-shirt, maybe scrounge some shorts," he unlocked the door to his apartment and led her up the stairs. And did his best not to picture how she'd look in them.

5

The result was far more incredible than he'd imagined. Her narrow shoulders made his "Firefighters Bring the Heat" ride low and expose a lot of neck and collar. Even though it was his longest one, it rode barely past her hips. A pair of gym shorts revealed long, powerful legs.

He did his best to hide his astonishment with a cough and knew he'd completely failed. He enjoyed strong competent women…if he didn't, he was on the wrong crew. Candace had drawn more than the standard share of women to her team—one or two women was still the exception on a twenty-person IHC, and they had five. But not a one was like the dark-haired soldier standing in the middle of his small living room.

"You want to do it, I don't mind."

"Want to?" He gasped it out on a half laugh. How could a man *not* want to; she was stunning. Randall didn't know what self control had him walking up to her, placing his hands on her shoulders, and looking her right in the eyes. "Let me know when *you* want to. Then we'll talk."

He waited for that odd processing lag that she had. Finally she just nodded and turned for the couch. He got out of there before she bent over to adjust the blanket and made the t-shirt ride up higher than it already did. Besides, he'd seen the size of the handgun she'd slipped under her pillow.

6

*S*heila stayed on the couch that first night and puzzled at Randall's comment. What did *she* want? There was the thousand-dollar question.

The door to what she wanted had been closed. The Army offered to let her stay in if she would drive domestic, but no foreign action. She'd told them just how far out of the daylight they could ram it. Their ever-so knowing and tolerant smiles—they'd all read her psych profile after all—almost earned them a personal demonstration. The black ops contractors didn't need drivers, they needed operators —she'd checked. As far as "want" went, she hadn't looked any further than that.

Three more days and nights with Randall didn't add a lot of clarity. During the days they went on long cold hikes through the crisp mountain air. In the evenings, they'd sometimes meet up with a few of the others in a locals' bar —the kind of place she'd been trying to find that first night —or they'd end up back at his apartment playing backgammon or watching some action flick.

Sunday night, end of the weekend, she went to lie on

the couch when the first bit of *want* seeped into her brain. She didn't care about the sex one way or the other, but it would be nice to be held. What was more, it would be nice to be held by Randall. Somehow all the care she had to take to not be offensive to civilians didn't matter around him.

For once not thinking deeply, she turned aside and followed him through his bedroom door. She'd checked out the place the first day, had the layout clear in her head (including all exits), and could walk right to the bed in the pitch dark.

When she slipped under the covers, it earned her a grunt of surprise, but no more. She lay against him. For a long frozen moment he lay perfectly still unsure what to do next—it was a moment she knew well. He didn't paw at her or jump her, both of which she was ready for; just part of the price.

Instead, he pulled her in and held on tight.

Somehow he knew that this was what she wanted. No, he wasn't some freaking telepath like those damned Army psychs thought they were. Randall waited while she figured out what she wanted. For a long time, it was exactly what he was giving her.

When she decided it was more, he seemed pretty okay with that as well.

7

Randall knew he was dreaming, but four weeks hadn't been enough to wake him up so far and he was starting to hope it never would. Just as she had that first night, Sheila had started on the periphery, staying in town when he went to work on the Monday after Thanksgiving. That had lasted her active nature about two days.

By the end of the week she had fully integrated into the small business that he and Patsy had set up with Jess and Jill. WUI Cleaners—the name made them laugh even if no one else seemed to get the joke. They specialized in cleaning up the Wildland-Urban Interface around homes, securing them as well as possible against the dangers of wildfire. They dropped dead trees, or ones too close to a house. Around homes pushed into thickly wooded areas, they trimmed off all of the dead lower branches that could act as ladder fuels to take a fire from ground to crown. They'd recently expanded from burn piles into prescribed burns, clearing brush and deadwood from the forest floor with carefully controlled small fires.

Sheila—still oblivious to the cold—started out dragging branches and tending burn piles. It wasn't long before she picked up saw work and finally harness work climbing in the trees. The general lack of snow let them keep busy in Leavenworth, only occasionally shifting down the dry eastern slopes of the Cascades to Cashmere or Wenatchee.

She didn't really open up around the others, but her hesitations shortened over time. They'd talked about the whole TBI thing, looked up the symptoms together, and it didn't quite fit.

"As you just demonstrated, it's not that you think any slower than I do," Randall observed one night as they lay exhausted together. A good work day around the Kitchner farm, followed by an equally thorough workout with only a short break for delivery pizza in bed. Slow thinking was one of the main signs of a traumatic brain injury and Sheila had shifted over the month from an active lover to an immensely creative one. Combined with her magnificent body, he was a complete goner.

Her silence was her usual answer but he could feel her listening. She was like that when they were making love as well, completely silent but gloriously present.

"It's more like we're all speaking a foreign language and you need time to translate it."

She buried her face against his shoulder for a while before finally responding, "God, I hope you're right. It feels that way. Even as familiar as you feel, there's a strangeness I can't seem to get around."

"Familiar, huh?"

8

Sheila could hear the tease, but she could feel the pain.

Randall felt so much more than "familiar" but she didn't know how to say it. He had welcomed her into his world with no questions asked. A dinner, his couch, his bed, his job, his life.

And what had she offered in return? Her body. There should be more than that.

She considered using it to demonstrate quite how much more than familiar he felt. But it wasn't that simple or that crass…because it *was* more than that.

"You feel…"

And he waited while she searched for the word. It wasn't that sluggish feeling she'd felt back when the Army was giving her the medical discharge. It wasn't even the foreignness issue, though that was the best explanation she'd heard of it.

"I feel…" That was the real problem. Her feelings—other than anger at what had happened, at the raghead who'd blown up her truck, with her inability to say what she meant—were distant, almost vague. She didn't know what she felt and had no idea how to put words to that.

So, she fell back on showing it with her body. But it wasn't merely great sex this time. It was more. It was deeper. She groaned aloud as the layers of defense broke loose inside her. Randall eased his way past more than the barricades of the flesh, he also shattered the massive walls she'd built around her own emotions without realizing.

This time, as her body shuddered with pleasure, it wasn't a release. It was a cleansing.

9

———————

The fire hit and it hit hard. December had been unseasonably dry, less than a foot of snow and a series of warm afternoons that had melted what little fell. The town had brought in snowmaking machines so that they could have a white Christmas.

Patsy's call wrenched them out of deep sleep. Just breaking dawn outside the window.

"We're activated. Move!" And she was gone. Hotshot teams were never mobilized in mid-winter.

He punched Tori's number, remembered that she was wintering with her famous writer husband in Seattle, mumbled an apology for waking her, and hung up. Next on his leg of the phone tree…nobody who was still in town.

Time to move.

He was pulling on his cotton long johns as Sheila stripped off her t-shirt and began doing the same.

"What are you doing?" Other than escalating the hell out of his pulse rate. Not in a hundred years could he get used to the look of her.

"There's a fire." No hesitation at all. No question either.

"You're not…"

He stopped when he saw her baleful gaze.

…a firefighter. Though he'd trained her in all he could and she'd learned fast, she wasn't trained for wildfire—didn't have her Incident Qualification System "red card." However, he'd long since learned that changing Sheila Williams' mind once she set it was not something that mortal men should attempt. There was no hesitation when she was in work mode. The same thing had happened when they were working for WUI Cleaners. When there was action, Sheila didn't pause for a microsecond. No more wrong with her brain than her stunning body.

Fine. Let Candace try to face her down about the "official" certification.

He watched her pulling on the Nomex fire retardant gear he'd given her as a gift when she'd proved she was going to stick with WUI for a while. A powerful woman climbing into firefighting gear. And not just any woman, but Sheila Williams.

Randall knew what he wanted to see for the rest of his days, and he was looking right at it.

"You're still naked," she said without looking up from lacing her boots.

"Shit!" He finished dressing at firefighter speed.

When they arrived at the station, Candace took one look at Sheila and growled, "I don't have time to argue this shit. Fine. You're attached to Randall's hip. I find you more than ten feet apart, I'm gonna kick your ass off the fire and out of this town."

Then she turned to him, "She dies, it's totally on you." Then she rushed off to ream someone else's ass about something.

"Wipe the surprise off your face, Randall." Sheila gave him a gentle shove to get him into motion. "Let's go."

He led her to the type 3 wildfire engine that hadn't seen a job since October. Built on a truck frame, it carried five people, five hundred gallons of water, and could blast a hundred-and-fifty gallons per minute out of fifteen-hundred feet of hose. The big diesel, rear dualies, and four-wheel drive also meant it could cross over seriously rough terrain.

Sheila went for the driver's door, then stopped with her hand on the handle. "Sorry, old habits." She circled to the passenger side.

Randall had learned that it was easier to just let her drive the work truck, but there were special insurance issues here and he was glad that he didn't have to force it.

Captain Cantrell came by and slapped an address in his hand. "Remote as hell. None of my engines can make it up there. It's up to your team to lead. My men are right behind you."

Randall could see teams of firefighters loading the backs of their four-wheel drive personal vehicles with fire gear and piling aboard. Jess, Candace, and Patsy slid into the back seat of his truck's cab. It was odd having Sheila in Tori's usual seat beside him, not that he was complaining.

Jill actually chirped the tires on the other wildland engine as she pulled out ahead of him along with the rest of the Leavenworth Hotshots wintering in Leavenworth. Ten people. Half their normal crew. They'd need Cantrell's people fast. The problem was that though they were good guys, they were volunteers and would need to be watched like hawks. Along with Sheila…though he'd never found watching her to be a burden.

Together, he and Jill raced the big engines down Highway 2 toward the small town of Dryden.

10

Sheila wasn't ready for the scale of a wildfire or the scale of the change that washed over her easy-going and affable lover. She barely recognized him. Deep in a valley beyond Dryden, a fire was ripping apart the landscape.

"Goddamn winter hunters," his unexpected snarl came from deep in his chest.

"What's wrong with hunters?"

"They're big on exploding targets. Doesn't matter that the damned things are outlawed on state forest land; they love seeing the flash and bang during target practice. Then, if they start a fire, the hunters scram so that they don't get caught and have to pay for the firefight. Not the primary cause of our manmade fires, but it's climbing."

"What are the primaries?"

"Campfires and arsonists. But there aren't any hiking trails back here and arsonists like showier fires than the back hill country. There also hasn't been any lightning lately, which says numbskull hunters. They were probably bored because the elk are staying in the higher pastures due to the mildness of the season." Randall sounded seriously pissed. Army-style pissed, something Sheila didn't know he had in him.

She was already discovering a soft-spot in her head for Randall Jones; this just amped up the developing pile of mush that was her brain. She'd *never* been mushy about a man or anything else before—except maybe her truck before the roadside bomb dismembered it. Actually, she cared more about him than anything before which was a surprise. If you'd asked her a month ago, she'd have said she was past caring about anything ever again.

They swooped off the end of the gravel road they'd been following into the backcountry and the big truck jounced and jostled as he headed into an area that was a combination of meadow and trees. All conifers—mostly scattered—except low in the valley, where the water would accumulate. They made thick clumps down there. Higher on the dry slopes they spread out, and the brown grasses dominated. The fire was climbing both valley walls simultaneously and sending a plume of smoke soaring upward like a line of JDAM bombs. She kept expecting to feel the shockwave slam into the truck. But the smoke just kept rolling upward in a continuous gray sheet, dark with ash above and bright with flames below.

"Flanks first," Candace called from the back of the truck as Randall slammed it to a halt over two hundred yards away from the fire. Everyone piled out of the back.

"What are they…" Then Sheila stopped asking. Stay in the truck. Watch and learn, just like in the Army.

The firefighters who piled out of the two trucks spread out in a short line. In moments they were swinging their Pulaski fire axes, digging a line across the meadow. Great clumps of grass and dirt were peeled up. They moved in a fast, coordinated action.

The townie firefighters drove up and were soon put to the same task with varying degrees of effectiveness. Just like a fresh shipment of boot camp privates arriving on the line, the main thing they did was make it really clear how skilled the hotshots were at what they did.

Randall dropped the wildland engine into four-wheel low and continued toward the fire until she thought he was going to drive straight into it. She could see Jill in the other engine driving down into the valley ahead of the fire and climbing back up the other side.

The smoke was thicker here. They were close enough that she could see the fire crawling up the trees like a living thing. It crept through the grass beneath the trees, like an orange serpent until it reached the next tree and then raced upward: a flicker and a snap at first, but soon a rush high into the boughs. He drove along the front as if it was no more than a guardrail on the highway. At the end, he turned along the flank, the truck tipping ten degrees sideways due to the grade.

"Here. Take over the wheel." Randall slid out the uphill-side door and closed it, even though the truck was still idling forward. By the time she slid across, he had fifty feet of one-inch hose pulled off the back and connected to the on-board pump.

"Just roll ahead slow," he spoke calmly over the radio.

"Sheila better not be driving my truck," Candace called back in response from her position on the front line.

Randall shot her a grin and Sheila decided that they'd both ignore her.

Sheila had to flex her hands a few times before she could bring herself to grab onto the steering wheel.

Randall walked up to the fire, the flames off the deep grass were as tall as he was. With a casual flick of his wrist, he opened the nozzle and began spraying the fire down.

She was surprised at how easily the flames died. It took her a while to see why. Randall ignored the black area that had already been burned. He concentrated only on the burning line which was truly not very wide. Whenever he reached a tree burning along the line, he'd spray it for an extra moment to kill the fire, but never slowed.

As she became oriented to his world, she learned more of what to watch. In the rearview mirror, she saw a patch still smoking. She tapped the horn and pointed back when Randall looked at her. He slashed the spray at the smoke, thoroughly inundating it, then continued ahead without breaking stride.

He was so clearly in his element. She appreciated the casual skill with which he and the others of WUI had dealt with everything. But watching him have the same attitude toward an active fire was a real sight to see. He might not be Army, but that didn't stop her from feeling better just for being in his presence.

Over the next hour they traveled a couple of times down to the stream at the bottom of the valley and pumped aboard another five-hundred gallons.

"It's a surreal place. We call it The Black," Randall explained as he rode easily in the passenger seat while she climbed the engine back up the slope through the burned-out char to the fire line. "Part of the natural life cycle in this kind of environment. The grass and the trees know what to do; we're the problem. There are power lines over that ridge," he pointed one way. "And homes over that one," he pointed the other. "So we have to kill it off even though it's just a baby fire."

"Just a baby?"

"I half think the Captain must have been bored to call us out on this one. Maybe he knew Candace was getting antsy; she's always happiest when she's fighting a fire. Doesn't matter. We'll kill it in plenty of time for dinner."

Once they had the flanks doused, Randall drove the truck around to the head, trading with Sheila because he figured he shouldn't flaunt in Candace's face who'd actually been driving all morning.

The crew had been busy and had a long line sliced through the soil. The trench ran twenty feet wide and from his flank, all the way down to the creek, and well up the other side.

"Spray the line behind us," Candace instructed when he pulled up. The look she gave him said that switching drivers hadn't fooled her for a second no matter how hard Sheila tried to look innocent in the passenger seat.

"Sure," Randall eyed the grassy slope beyond the trench. "Just as soon as you get these amateurs to move their vehicles."

Candace looked over her shoulder and swore. His path was blocked by a tangled array of the volunteer firefighters parked far too close to the line. It only took moments before she had firefighters racing off the line to move their vehicles. Totally overestimating the danger, the volunteers then drove five-hundred yards away. It would take them a while to trudge their way back.

"Better light the backfire soon," he nodded toward the nearly empty line now manned by only a half dozen hotshots along its half-mile length.

The fire head wasn't more than a few hundred feet away and was going to arrive at the line before the stray volunteers did.

A backfire had to be lit right now on the fire-side of the trench they'd cut. Unable to cross the trench, it would slowly burn up the fuels back toward the main fire, robbing it of heat before it hit the line.

"Shit!" Candace got on the radio to the other hotshots and raced off to start the fire.

"Darn it!" Jill's voice came over the radio. She really was too sweet, though with Sheila beside him he was no longer wishing she had a twin sister.

"What?" Candace's voice was harsh, in no mood for additional problems as she sprinted to gather up her own fire torch to ignite the line.

"I'm in the creek," Jill called. "Stuck trying to get back to your side."

Randall looked down the slope and saw the big red engine down in the bottom of the valley. The fire was still running hot through the trees, headed her way. This first fireline was only to get the fire off the slopes. The second battle would be down in the those trees, so there was nothing set up there yet to protect her.

He slammed into gear and raced down the hill toward her, barely remembering to warn Sheila to hang on before he slammed over a foot-thick fallen tree.

"I stuck it good," Jill called out as he drove up. She already had a length of chain hooked up to her front bumper, but the slope was steep and he wouldn't have a lot of extra power to pull her free while trying to climb. Hopefully it would be enough because she was wheel deep in creek water and the fire was on the move.

He backed down as close as he dared, already feeling the first of the fire's heat through the window. Jill shot him a thumbs up as soon as she had the chain hooked up and raced back to her truck.

They eased into first gear together, but it wasn't budging. The fire wasn't going to give him time to unhook, circle around, and try pulling her back the other way.

Sheila cursed from beside him and then was gone with a slam of her door.

He didn't have time to deal with whatever snit-fit she was having. In the rearview mirror he kept an eye on Jill in the stuck fire engine's driver's seat as they tried once more to dislodge it without success.

The warmth of the fire was now up to a hot summer's day and climbing fast. Even with both engines pumping, the flames would be too big to fight directly.

Then, shortly before he was going to call her to abandon her engine, he saw Sheila stalk up to Jill's driver-side door. She yanked it open and, with little ceremony, shoved Jill over into the passenger seat.

"Give me five feet of slack," her terse command snapped over the radio.

Randall glanced once at the flames. He should call for them to abandon the engine. There would barely be time to undo the chain and get the hell out.

"Don't think. Do it!"

Randall smiled to himself as he eased off the chain. That sounded just like his Sheila.

She began rocking the truck back and forth in the creek. The slick rocks gave her little purchase, but she was getting some motion as she slammed back and forth between drive and reverse.

"On five. Give me everything you've got, Randall."

He shoved in the clutch, shifted into first, and revved the engine. It had better work on five because by ten the fire would overrun both of them. It was a small enough fire to ride it out inside the engines, but it would be hard on the engines themselves.

Sheila counted down her increasing rocking motion.

Her shout of "Now!" came just halfway between a rear swing and a forward one.

Anticipating her, he came off the clutch hard and slammed down on the gas.

The five feet of slack jerked out of the chain, jarring him hard against his seatbelt.

He kept his foot down and the big diesel groaned with power.

As if the creek didn't want to let go, the other engine emerged a foot at a time, sheeting water to the sides.

There was a moment when their momentum hung in the balance as grass and mud sprayed off their spinning tires, but his front pair found some traction on good soil and it was enough to drag them both forward and up the slope.

He checked the rearview and watched as a burning tree crashed down where the engine had been stuck just moments before.

"That felt good," Sheila couldn't stop saying it. "That felt soooo good."

"Hey!" Randall complained. "You're only supposed to be saying that about me."

Sheila grabbed Randall and shoved his back against the rear wall of the fire station. He stopped complaining when she kissed him. The joy that coursed through her ran deep and hot and she poured it into the kiss.

His strong arms clamped tight around her just as they had that first night she'd climbed into his bed. Except now it wasn't about being held—it was all about who was holding her.

"You don't feel good, Randall," she nibbled at his neck, making him squirm. "You feel incredible!"

He laughed at her crow of delight.

"Will you two cut it out?" Candace stuck her head out the back door of the equipment bay. "We can hear you right through the wall."

"Nope," Sheila had no intention of stopping with Randall any time soon.

Candace looked at her watch. "I figure you have one hour to get home, shower, and get back here after picking up the pies at Sam's place. Get a move on, I don't like my pies or my hotshots to be late." And she slammed the door.

Randall laughed and tried to pull her back into a kiss, but she held off.

Her mental processes really weren't slow. They didn't feel slow anyway. Maybe that was all part of the issue. But she'd heard something that…

"Did Candace just say '*hotshots*'? Plural?"

Randall sobered and turned to study the closed door.

Then she felt his shrug.

"Could be…"

The shower was fun as always.

Sheila almost felt shy sharing it with the firefighter that Randall had turned into, but shy had never been a thing between them. Still, now that she knew the hard-core firefighter that lurked beneath his easy-going demeanor, it was like she was with someone else. Someone even better than she'd thought she was with, which was astonishing as she'd been counting herself damned lucky of late.

And Randall got her to smile as they went into the Bavarian Bakery to pick up the pies for dinner; the place was such classic German kitsch. But the sample cinnamon rugelach they'd split had been splendidly authentic.

It was so different walking through town now than it had been a month ago. It didn't matter that the snow was artificial; the town glittered with tiny ice crystals. The polka band was in full swing as were the chaotic crowds of children. She managed to dodge all collisions this time, so there would be no test of their reaction to her—something she still wasn't ready for.

"Damn, I keep forgetting to buy twinkle lights."

He hesitated in front of the Christmas store window, and she didn't even cringe.

"When I told my sister that I was in love, she said I should get some twinkle lights for the bedroom," he set off walking again.

"When you told your sister…*what?*" Sheila ground to a halt. *In love?* Some chattering tourist couple slammed into her from behind and bounced off.

Randall simply smiled at her. "I think making love to you by the light of twinkle lights would be a very good thing."

"No. What's that other thing you said?"

"See? I told you there weren't any issues with your reaction time," he kissed her on the nose and then kept walking toward the fire station with his armful of pie boxes.

Sheila wasn't used to having to scramble to keep up with a man.

Luke came out of a side street not a dozen steps ahead. There were some things that she definitely wasn't going to discuss in front of *him*.

Or at all.

And the crowd built from there.

Or was she?

By the time they reached the fire station, more firefighters and families had joined them. They all greeted her by name, made her feel welcome. Sheila realized that she knew all of their names as well. Had eaten at several of their houses. Knew most of the kids' names too. *When did that happen?*

With no privacy, she could only puzzle at Randall's statement. The problem was that the more she did, the less strange it became. She cared for Randall. She really did. Is that what love felt like? If it was, how in hell was she supposed to know.

It was halfway through the dinner before she was able to track down Candace and ask her what that "hotshots" comment had meant.

"One of the main things I look for when I'm building my hotshot team is what you showed today."

"What's that?"

"You're not afraid of fire. You keep thinking even when it's right on top of you. Damned hard to test that without a real fire."

Sheila had driven through enough shellings and bombardment that the fire hadn't fazed her at all. "What are the other things?"

"Saving my damned engine," Candace grinned at her. "Work with Randall, get your red card. Tryouts are in the spring, not that you need to worry about that." She punched Sheila on the arm like guys did and strutted back into the crowd. It was no longer a surprise that she had married a Navy SEAL and was keeping him happy.

It was only at the end of the night, as she and Randall were walking arm in arm back through the sleeping village that Sheila really connected that this was Christmas Eve…she checked the cuckoo clock in the window of Der Markt Platz…no, Christmas Day. She'd known it was close. Obligatory call with Mom about whether or not she was coming home for it, etc. etc. But the firehall dinner had just been a Christmas party. Not the official Eve of.

"I didn't get you anything, Randall. Please tell me that you didn't get me a present either."

He looked aside as if seeking a subject change.

"Oh no! What did you get me? Are there any shops open past midnight?" The empty street answered that one.

"Maybe McDonald's up on the highway is open and I could get you some French fries."

Now he seemed to be the one having trouble connecting words. After a few slowing paces, he turned and led her away from the shops to the small park where the band had been playing Christmas carols earlier. She could still hear them on the night air. That should have reminded her to get him something, would have if they hadn't been playing them since the moment of her arrival back at Thanksgiving.

He led her to the little gazebo and sat beside her on the bench.

"I got you something," his voice was low and rough. "Probably pretty damned stupid, but..." His shrug showed his sudden unease.

"Just, I don't know, just give it to me and I'll get you something equally stupid when the stores reopen. Then we'll be even." It came out in a mad rush. She didn't know why she was feeling so nervous. It wasn't like her.

"Equally stupid?" There was a tease in his voice that she'd come to like. There was never a hidden agenda behind it; it was more his way of laughing with her rather than at her. And he took her return teases in stride just as easily as he took her silences.

"I promise," Sheila raised her right hand. "Equally stupid."

"Okay," he blew out a hard huff of breath that made a brief cloud in the chill air. He dug into a pocket, pulled out a small box, and opened it.

Inside was a golden ring with a small ruby the color of fire. "It's beautiful. Simple and perfect."

"It's yours, if you want it."

"Of course I do, it's—" and with those words her brain seized up.

I do? Randall hadn't offered her a present. Well, not a present like a present present. Her brain was babbling.

She looked up into his dark eyes and studied him carefully by the soft street lighting. He didn't look away. Didn't shy off.

"You said to just give it to you," he explained. "I had a speech, which I can't remember. I'll kneel if you'd like. But the important part is that every one of my days has been better for having you in it. I'm betting that isn't going to change. I know it won't."

Sheila wanted to protest that she was a wreck, but she didn't feel like one. Not when Randall was around. She felt capable, strong…

She looked at the ring once more. It wasn't as simple as it had first appeared. The band was twisted, like a mobius strip. All one side, the inside becoming the outside and the outside in. It was an elegant piece of work.

And it was who she was, all twisted up, the inside and the outside blurred until they became one because of the man waiting patiently beside her.

Well, not altogether patiently. She knew him well enough to see the strain, but he'd never pushed her to be other than who she was. That's when she knew that the ring wasn't the gift, Randall Jones was. A life-long sized gift.

She leaned forward and kissed him lightly.

"Something equally stupid…" she whispered against his lips. "I promise. I really do."

Candace Cantrell and Luke Rawlings may have been the heart of the team, but I think it was in the final story of Sheila Williams that my writing changed the most.

The Firehawks Hotshots—and the companion Firehawks Lookouts series—had let me experiment with romantic suspense tales in the short form of stories. They were fun, lively, and interesting to write.

But it was Sheila's story where I feel I first captured a glimpse of the other side of war. My friend Suzanne Brockmann says that she almost never shows her heroes in a war zone because she refuses to pretty it up. I have made a different choice, showing bits of the battles' challenge and terror, without showing its moments of horror. It has helped me as a person to better understand the warriors I write about.

In Sheila I explored the huge challenges that make it so hard for our warriors when they come home. I've written more of those tales since (most notably *NSDQ*, *Reaching Out at Henderson's Ranch*, and *When They Just Know*) and more are planned. Sheila brought a degree of realism to my writing that I feel has carried through ever since.

When I delve into a new character, I can feel Sheila watching me closely to make sure I look deeper and make a greater effort to find what lies underneath the shield that a true warrior keeps so firmly in place.

I'm trying, Sheila. I'm trying.

WILDFIRE AT DAWN
(EXCERPT)

WILDFIRE AT DAWN

(EXCERPT)

Mount Hood Aviation's lead smokejumper Johnny Akbar Jepps rolled out of his lower bunk careful not to bang his head on the upper. Well, he tried to roll out, but every muscle fought him, making it more a crawl than a roll. He checked the clock on his phone. Late morning.

He'd slept twenty of the last twenty-four hours and his body felt as if he'd spent the entire time in one position. The coarse plank flooring had been worn smooth by thousands of feet hitting exactly this same spot year in and year out for decades. He managed to stand upright...then he felt it, his shoulders and legs screamed.

Oh, right.

The New Tillamook Burn. Just about the nastiest damn blaze he'd fought in a decade of jumping wildfires. Two hundred thousand acres—over three hundred square miles—of rugged Pacific Coast Range forest, poof! The worst forest fire in a decade for the Pacific Northwest, but they'd killed it off without a single fatality or losing a single town. There'd been a few bigger ones, out in the flatter eastern part of Oregon state. But that much area—mostly on terrain too steep to climb even when it wasn't on fire—had been a horror.

Akbar opened the blackout curtain and winced against the summer brightness of blue sky and towering trees that lined the firefighter's camp. Tim was gone from the upper bunk, without kicking Akbar on his way out. He must have been as hazed out as Akbar felt.

He did a couple of side stretches and could feel every single minute of the eight straight days on the wildfire to contain the bastard, then the excruciating nine days more to convince it that it was dead enough to hand off to a Type II incident mop-up crew. Not since his beginning days on a hotshot crew had he spent seventeen days on a single fire.

And in all that time nothing more than catnaps in the acrid safety of the "black"—the burned-over section of a fire, black with char and stark with no hint of green foliage. The mop-up crews would be out there for weeks before it was dead past restarting, but at least it was truly done in. That fire wasn't merely contained; they'd killed it bad.

Yesterday morning, after demobilizing, his team of smokies had pitched into their bunks. No wonder he was so damned sore. His stretches worked out the worst of the kinks but he still must be looking like an old man stumbling about.

He looked down at the sheets. Damn it. They'd been fresh before he went to the fire, now he'd have to wash them again. He'd been too exhausted to shower before sleeping and they were all smeared with the dirt and soot that he could still feel caking his skin. Two-Tall Tim, his number two man and as tall as two of Akbar, kinda, wasn't in his bunk. His towel was missing from the hook.

Shower. Shower would be good. He grabbed his own

towel and headed down the dark, narrow hall to the far end of the bunk house. Every one of the dozen doors of his smoke teams were still closed, smokies still sacked out. A glance down another corridor and he could see that at least a couple of the Mount Hood Aviation helicopter crews were up, but most still had closed doors with no hint of light from open curtains sliding under them. All of MHA had gone above and beyond on this one.

"Hey, Tim." Sure enough, the tall Eurasian was in one of the shower stalls, propped up against the back wall letting the hot water stream over him.

"Akbar the Great lives," Two-Tall sounded half asleep.

"Mostly. Doghouse?" Akbar stripped down and hit the next stall. The old plywood dividers were flimsy with age and gray with too many showers. The Mount Hood Aviation firefighters' Hoodie One base camp had been a kids' summer camp for decades. Long since defunct, MHA had taken it over and converted the playfields into landing areas for their helicopters, and regraded the main road into a decent airstrip for the spotter and jump planes.

"Doghouse? Hell, yeah. I'm like ten thousand calories short." Two-Tall found some energy in his voice at the idea of a trip into town.

The Doghouse Inn was in the nearest town. Hood River lay about a half hour down the mountain and had exactly what they needed: smokejumper-sized portions and a very high ratio of awesomely fit young women come to windsurf the Columbia Gorge. The Gorge, which formed the Washington and Oregon border, provided a fantastically target-rich environment for a smokejumper too long in the woods.

"You're too tall to be short of anything," Akbar knew he was being a little slow to reply, but he'd only been awake for minutes.

"You're like a hundred thousand calories short of being even a halfway decent size," Tim was obviously recovering faster than he was.

"Just because my parents loved me instead of tying me to a rack every night ain't my problem, buddy."

He scrubbed and soaped and scrubbed some more until he felt mostly clean.

"I'm telling you, Two-Tall. Whoever invented the hot shower, that's the dude we should give the Nobel prize to."

"You say that every time."

"You arguing?"

He heard Tim give a satisfied groan as some muscle finally let go under the steamy hot water. "Not for a second."

Akbar stepped out and walked over to the line of sinks, smearing a hand back and forth to wipe the condensation from the sheet of stainless steel screwed to the wall. His hazy reflection still sported several smears of char.

"You so purdy, Akbar."

"Purdier than you, Two-Tall." He headed back into the shower to get the last of it.

"So not. You're jealous."

Akbar wasn't the least bit jealous. Yes, despite his lean height, Tim was handsome enough to sweep up any ladies he wanted.

But on his own, Akbar did pretty damn well himself. What he didn't have in height, he made up for with a proper smokejumper's muscled build. Mixed with his tan-dark Indian complexion, he did fine.

The real fun, of course, was when the two of them went cruising together. The women never knew what to make of the two of them side by side. The contrast kept them off balance enough to open even more doors.

He smiled as he toweled down. It also didn't hurt that

their opening answer to "what do you do" was "I jump out of planes to fight forest fires."

Worked every damn time. God he loved this job.

***

THE SMALL TOWN of Hood River, a winding half-an-hour down the mountain from the MHA base camp, was hopping. Mid-June, colleges letting out. Students and the younger set of professors high-tailing it to the Gorge. They packed the bars and breweries and sidewalk cafes. Suddenly every other car on the street had a windsurfing board tied on the roof.

The snooty rich folks were up at the historic Timberline Lodge on Mount Hood itself, not far in the other direction from MHA. Down here it was a younger, thrill seeker set and you could feel the energy.

There were other restaurants in town that might have better pickings, but the Doghouse Inn was MHA tradition and it was a good luck charm—no smokie in his right mind messed with that. This was the bar where all of the MHA crew hung out. It didn't look like much from the outside, just a worn old brick building beaten by the Gorge's violent weather. Aged before its time, which had been long ago.

But inside was awesome. A long wooden bar stretched down one side with a half-jillion microbrew taps and a small but well-stocked kitchen at the far end. The dark wood paneling, even on the ceiling, was barely visible beneath thousands of pictures of doghouses sent from patrons all over the world. Miniature dachshunds in ornately decorated shoeboxes, massive Newfoundlands in backyard mansions that could easily house hundreds of their smaller kin, and everything in between. A gigantic

Snoopy atop his doghouse in full Red Baron fighting gear dominated the far wall. Rumor said Shulz himself had been here two owners before and drawn it.

Tables were grouped close together, some for standing and drinking, others for sitting and eating.

"Amy, sweetheart!" Two-Tall called out as they entered the bar. The perky redhead came out from behind the bar to receive a hug from Tim. Akbar got one in turn, so he wasn't complaining. Cute as could be and about his height; her hugs were better than taking most women to bed. Of course, Gerald the cook and the bar's co-owner was big enough and strong enough to squish either Tim or Akbar if they got even a tiny step out of line with his wife. Gerald was one amazingly lucky man.

Akbar grabbed a Walking Man stout and turned to assess the crowd. A couple of the air jocks were in. Carly and Steve were at a little table for two in the corner, obviously not interested in anyone's company but each others. Damn, that had happened fast. New guy on the base swept up one of the most beautiful women on the planet. One of these days he'd have to ask Steve how he'd done that. Or maybe not. It looked like they were settling in for the long haul; the big "M" was so not his own first choice.

Carly was also one of the best FBANs in the business. Akbar was a good Fire Behavior Analyst, had to be or he wouldn't have made it to first stick—lead smokie of the whole MHA crew. But Carly was something else again. He'd always found the Flame Witch, as she was often called, daunting and a bit scary besides; she knew the fire better than it did itself. Steve had latched on to one seriously driven lady. More power to him.

The selection of female tourists was especially good today, but no other smokies in yet. They'd be in soon enough…most of them had groaned awake and said they were coming as he and Two-Tall kicked their hallway doors, but not until they'd been on their way out—he and Tim had first pick. Actually some of the smokies were coming, others had told them quite succinctly where they could go—but hey, jumping into fiery hell is what they did for a living anyway, so no big change there.

A couple of the chopper pilots had nailed down a big table right in the middle of the bustling seating area: Jeannie, Mickey, and Vern. Good "field of fire" in the immediate area.

He and Tim headed over, but Akbar managed to snag the chair closest to the really hot lady with down-her-back curling dark-auburn hair at the next table over—set just right to see her profile easily. Hard shot, sitting there with her parents, but damn she was amazing. And if that was her mom, it said the woman would be good looking for a long time to come.

Two-Tall grimaced at him and Akbar offered him a comfortable "beat out your ass" grin. But this one didn't feel like that. Maybe it was the whole parental thing. He sat back and kept his mouth shut.

He made sure that Two-Tall could see his interest. That made Tim honor bound to try and cut Akbar out of the running.

Laura Jenson had spotted them coming into the restaurant. Her dad was only moments behind.

"Those two are walking like they just climbed off their first-ever horseback ride."

She had to laugh, they did. So stiff and awkward they barely managed to move upright. They didn't look like first-time windsurfers, aching from the unexpected workout. They'd also walked in like they thought they were two gifts to god, which was even funnier. She turned away to avoid laughing in their faces. Guys who thought like that rarely appreciated getting a reality check.

Available at fine retailers everywhere.

ABOUT THE AUTHOR

M.L. Buchman started the first of over 60 novels, 100 short stories, and a fast-growing pile of audiobooks while flying from South Korea to ride his bicycle across the Australian Outback. Part of a solo around the world trip that ultimately launched his writing career in: thrillers, military romantic suspense, contemporary romance, and SF/F.

Recently named in *The 20 Best Romantic Suspense Novels: Modern Masterpieces* by ALA's Booklist, they have also selected his works three times as "Top-10 Romance Novel of the Year." His thrillers have been praised noting, "Tom Clancy fans will clamor for more."

As a 30-year project manager with a geophysics degree who has: designed and built houses, flown and jumped out of planes, and solo-sailed a 50' ketch, he is awed by what's possible. More at: www.mlbuchman.com.

Other works by M. L. Buchman: *(* - also in audio)*

Thrillers

Dead Chef
Swap Out!
One Chef!
Two Chef!

Miranda Chase
*Drone**
*Thunderbolt**
*Condor**

Romantic Suspense

Delta Force
*Target Engaged**
*Heart Strike**
*Wild Justice**
*Midnight Trust**

Firehawks
MAIN FLIGHT
Pure Heat
Full Blaze
*Hot Point**
*Flash of Fire**
Wild Fire

SMOKEJUMPERS
*Wildfire at Dawn**
*Wildfire at Larch Creek**
*Wildfire on the Skagit**

The Night Stalkers
MAIN FLIGHT
The Night Is Mine
I Own the Dawn
Wait Until Dark
Take Over at Midnight
Light Up the Night
Bring On the Dusk
By Break of Day

AND THE NAVY
Christmas at Steel Beach
Christmas at Peleliu Cove
WHITE HOUSE HOLIDAY
*Daniel's Christmas**
*Frank's Independence Day**
*Peter's Christmas**
*Zachary's Christmas**
*Roy's Independence Day**
*Damien's Christmas**
5E
Target of the Heart
Target Lock on Love
Target of Mine
Target of One's Own

Shadow Force: Psi
*At the Slightest Sound**
*At the Quietest Word**

White House Protection Force
*Off the Leash**
*On Your Mark**
*In the Weeds**

Contemporary Romance

Eagle Cove
Return to Eagle Cove
Recipe for Eagle Cove
Longing for Eagle Cove
Keepsake for Eagle Cove

Henderson's Ranch
*Nathan's Big Sky**
*Big Sky, Loyal Heart**
*Big Sky Dog Whisperer**

Love Abroad
Heart of the Cotswolds: England
Path of Love: Cinque Terre, Italy

Other works by M. L. Buchman:

Contemporary Romance (cont)

Where Dreams
Where Dreams are Born
Where Dreams Reside
Where Dreams Are of Christmas
Where Dreams Unfold
Where Dreams Are Written

Science Fiction / Fantasy

Deities Anonymous
Cookbook from Hell: Reheated
Saviors 101

Single Titles
The Nara Reaction
Monk's Maze
the Me and Elsie Chronicles

Non-Fiction

Strategies for Success
Managing Your Inner Artist/Writer
*Estate Planning for Authors**
Character Voice
*Narrate and Record Your Own
Audiobook**

Short Story Series by M. L. Buchman:

Romantic Suspense

Delta Force
Delta Force

Firehawks
The Firehawks Lookouts
The Firehawks Hotshots
The Firebirds

The Night Stalkers
The Night Stalkers
The Night Stalkers 5E
The Night Stalkers CSAR
The Night Stalkers Wedding Stories

US Coast Guard
US Coast Guard

White House Protection Force
White House Protection Force

Contemporary Romance

Eagle Cove
Eagle Cove

Henderson's Ranch
*Henderson's Ranch**

Where Dreams
Where Dreams

Thrillers

Dead Chef
Dead Chef

Science Fiction / Fantasy

Deities Anonymous
Deities Anonymous

Other
The Future Night Stalkers
Single Titles

SIGN UP FOR M. L. BUCHMAN'S NEWSLETTER TODAY

and receive:
Release News
Free Short Stories
a Free Book

Do it today. Do it now.
http://free-book.mlbuchman.com